THE SIGN OF THE SEVEN SINS

THE SIGN OF THE SEVEN SINS

WILLIAM LE QUEUX

Originally published in 1901.

Published by Wildside Press for release in countries where it is in the public domain.

Visit us online at wildsidepress.com.

INTRODUCTION
KARL WURF

William Le Queux (1864–1927) was a British journalist, novelist, and some-time diplomat, whose sensational tales of intrigue and espionage once captured a vast international readership. Born in London to Anglo-French parents, he spent part of his youth in France and Italy, experiences that later shaped his cosmopolitan settings and fascination with international conspiracy. Before turning to fiction, he worked as a journalist for the *Globe* and the *Daily Mail*, where his flair for dramatic narrative quickly found an eager audience.

Le Queux drew inspiration from Alexandre Dumas, Jules Verne, and the serialized feuilleton tradition, while also taking cues from the emerging detective story popularized by Edgar Allan Poe and Arthur Conan Doyle. He blended these influences into a hybrid form—part crime novel, part spy thriller, part romance—that reflected both the glamour and the anxieties of the late Victorian and Edwardian eras. In particular, his invasion narratives, which stoked fears of German militarism and espionage, foreshadowed the concerns of the First World War.

Though critics often dismissed his melodramatic plots, Le Queux occupies an important place in popular literature. His stories of glamorous settings, ruthless villains, and ordinary men and women caught in webs of danger helped define the conventions of the modern thriller. Later writers such as John Buchan and Ian Fleming would refine what he popularized.

Among his many works, five stand out as particularly representative: *The Great War in England in 1897* (1894), *The Invasion of 1910* (1906), *The Czar's Spy* (1905), *Secrets of the Foreign Office* (1903), and *The Poisoned Bullet* (1916).

The Sign of the Seven Sins belongs to the strand of his fiction that explores high society and moral peril, set against the glittering but treacherous world of continental Europe.

CHAPTER I
IS PURELY PERSONAL

No; I DARE NOT reveal everything here, lest I may be misjudged. The narrative is, to say the least, a strange one; so amazing, indeed, that had I not been one of the actual persons concerned therein I would never have believed that such things could be.

Yet these chapters of an eventful personal history, remarkable though they may appear, are nevertheless the truth, a combination of unusual circumstances which will be found startling and curious, idyllic and tragic. Reader, I would confess all if I dared, but each of us have skeletons in our cupboards, both you and I—for, alas! I am no exception to the general rule among women.

If compelled by natural instinct to suppress one single fact, I may also add that it has little or nothing to do with the circumstances herein related. It only concerns myself, and no woman cares to afford food for gossips at her own expense. Briefly, it is my intention to narrate plainly and straightforwardly all that occurred, in the hope that those who read may approach it with a perfectly open mind and afterwards adjudge me fairly, impartially, and without the prejudice attaching to one whose shortcomings are many, and whose actions have perhaps not always been tempered by wisdom.

My name is Carmela Rosselli. I am of Italian extraction, five-and-twenty years of age last December, and already—yes, I confess it freely—I was utterly world-weary. I am an only child. My mother, one of the Burnetts of Washington, married Romolo Annibale, Marchese di Pistoja, an impecunious member of the Florentine aristocracy, and after a childhood at Washington I was sent to the Convent of San Paolo della Croce at Florence to obtain my education. My mother's money enabled the Marchese to live in the reckless style befitting a gentleman of the Tuscan nobility, but, unfortunately for me, both my parents died when I was fifteen and left me in the care of a second cousin, a woman but a few years older than myself; kind-hearted, everything that was most American and womanly, and—everything most devoted to me.

Thus it was that at the age of eighteen I received the maternal kiss of the grave-eyed Mother Superior, Suor Maria, and all the good sisters in turn, and returned to Washington accompanied by my guardian, Ulrica Yorke.

Like myself, Ulrica was wealthy and, being smart and good-looking, did not want for admirers. Together we lived for several years amid that society, diplomatic and otherwise, which circles around the White House, until one rather dull afternoon in the fall she, Ulrica, made a most welcome suggestion:

"Carmela, I am ruined morally and physically. I feel that I want a complete change."

I suggested New York or Florida for the winter.

"No," she answered, "I feel that I must build up my constitution as well as my spirits. Europe is the only place,—say London for a month, Paris, Monte Carlo for January, then Rome till after Easter."

"To Europe!" I gasped.

"Why not?" she inquired. "You have money,—what there is left of it,—and we may just as well go to Europe for a year and enjoy ourselves as vegetate here."

"You are tired of Guy?" I observed.

She shrugged her well-formed shoulders, pursed her lips, and contemplated her rings.

"He has become too serious," she said simply.

"And you want to escape him?" I remarked. "Do you know, Ulrica, that I really believe he loves you?"

"Well, and if he does?"

"I thought you told me only a couple of months ago that he was the best looking man in Washington, and that you had utterly lost your heart to him?"

She laughed.

"I've lost it so many times that I began to believe that I don't possess that very useful portion of the human anatomy. But," she added, "you pity him, eh? My dear Carmela, you should never pity a man. None of them is really worth sympathy. Nineteen out of every twenty are ready to declare love to any good-looking woman with money. Remember your dearest Ernest."

Mention of that name caused me a twinge.

"I have forgotten him!" I cried hotly. "I have forgiven—all is of the past!"

She laughed again.

"And you will go to Europe with me?" she said. "You will go to commence life afresh? What a funny thing life is, isn't it?"

I responded in the affirmative. Truth to tell, I was glad of that opportunity to escape from scenes which daily reminded me of the man whom I loved.

Ulrica knew it, but she was careful to avoid all further mention of the grief that was wearing out my heart.

We sailed from New York, duly landed in Liverpool a week later, and the same night found ourselves at the Hotel Cecil in London.

I knew little of the English metropolis, but we discovered some friends of Ulrica's living out at South Kensington, and the month we passed in the city of smoke and fog—for it was November—was quite the reverse of dreary. I had always believed London to be a sad second edition of New York, but was agreeably surprised at the many nice people we met in the circle into which Ulrica's friends introduced us.

In continuation of our pilgrimage we went to Paris, and after a month there went South.

We were in the salon of the Grand Hotel at Nice on the night of our arrival when suddenly someone uttered my name. We both turned quickly, and to our surprise saw two men we knew quite well in Washington standing before us. One was Reginald Thorne, a dark-haired, more than usually good-looking youth of about twenty-two or so, while the other was Gerald Keppel, a thin, fair-mustached young man some seven years his senior, son of old Benjamin Keppel, the well-known Pittsburg millionaire. Gerald was an old friend, but the former I knew but slightly, having met him once or twice at dances, for in Washington he was among the chief of the eligibles.

"Why, my dear Miss Rosselli!" he cried enthusiastically as we shook hands, "I'm so awfully glad to meet you. I had no idea you were here. Gerald was here dining with me, and we caught sight of you through the glass doors."

"Then you're staying here?" I exclaimed.

"Yes, Gerald's staying with his gov'nor. He has a villa out at Fabron. Have you been here long?"

"We've arrived in Nice today," interposed Ulrica, "and we haven't found a single soul we knew until now. I feel sure you'll take pity upon our loneliness, Mr. Thorne, won't you?"

"Of course," he laughed. "I suppose you go to Monte?"

"You men think of nothing but roulette and dinners at the Paris," she responded reproachfully, adding: "But after all, should we be worse if we had no soul for gambling? Have you had any luck this season?"

"Can't complain," he smiled. "I've been staying over there ten days or so. Gerald has had quite a run of good fortune. The other night he won the maximum on the zero-trois three times."

"Congratulations, my dear Gerald," exclaimed Ulrica approvingly. "You shall both take us over one day and let us try our fortune—if Mr. Thorne is agreeable?"

"Delighted, I'm sure," answered the latter, glancing at me, and by the look he gave me I felt convinced that my suspicions aroused in Washington about a year before were not quite groundless,—in brief, that he admired me.

CHAPTER II
TELLS SOMETHING ABOUT LOVE

THE FAULT OF US women is that we so often over-esteem the value of our good looks. To my mind the possession of handsome toilettes is quite as essential to a woman's well-being and man's contentment as are personal attractions. A woman, however beautiful she may be, loses half her charm to men's eyes if she dresses dowdily or without taste. Nobody ever saw a really beautiful Parisienne. For the most part they are thin-nosed, thin-lipped, scraggy-necked, yellow-faced, and absolutely ugly, yet are they not, merely by reason of their chic in dress, the most attractive women in the world? I know that many will dissent from this estimate, but as my mirror tells me that I have a face more than commonly handsome, and as dozens of men have further endorsed the mute evidence of my toilet-glass, I can only confess that all my success and all my harmless flirtations have had their commencements in the attraction exercised by the dainty creations of my couturière. We hear much complaining among women that there are not a sufficient number of nice men to go round, but, after all, the woman who knows how to dress need have no lack of offers of marriage. American women can always be distinguished from the English, and it is certain that to their quiet smartness in frills and furbelows their success in the marriage mart is due.

Yes, there was no doubt that Reggie Thorne admired me. I had suspected it on the night when we had waltzed together at the Pendymans' and afterwards gossiped together over ices, but with a woman dance-flirtations are soon forgotten, and, truth to tell, I had forgotten him until our sudden and unexpected meeting.

"What awfully good luck we've met Gerald and Reggie," Ulrica said when half-an-hour later we were seated together in the privacy of our sitting-room. "Gerald, poor boy, was always a bit gone on me in Washington, and as for Reggie—well, he'll make an excellent cavalier for you. Even if Mother Grundy is dead and buried, it isn't very respectable to be constantly trotting over to Monte Carlo without male escort."

"You mean that they'll be a couple of useful males—eh?"

"Certainly. Their advent is quite providential. Some of Gerald's luck at the table may be reflected upon us. I should dearly like to make my expenses at Monte."

"So should I."

"There's no reason why we shouldn't," she went on confidently. "I know quite a lot of people who've won enough to pay for the whole trip to Europe."

"Reggie has money, hasn't he?"

"Of course. The old man was on Wall Street and died very comfortably off. All of it went to Reggie, with an annuity to his mother. Of course, he's spent a good deal since. A man doesn't live in Washington as he does, drive tandem, and all that sort of thing on nothing a year."

"They used to say that Gerald Keppel hadn't a dollar only what the old man allowed him monthly—and a most niggardly allowance, I've heard."

"That's quite possible, my dear Carmela," she answered. "But one's position might be a good deal worse than the only son of a millionaire. Old Benjamin is eccentric. I've met the old buffer several times. He's addicted to my pet abomination in a man—paper collars."

"Then you'll take Gerald as your cavalier, and allot Reggie to me?" I laughed.

"Yes. I'm self-sacrificing, am I not?"

She was in high spirits, for she had long ago fascinated Gerald Keppel, and now intended to make use of him as her escort to that Palace of Delight which somebody has suggested might be known by the Sign of the Seven Sins.

Ulrica was a typical woman of the up-to-date type, pretty, with soft, wavy chestnut hair, and a pair of brown eyes that had attracted a host of men who had bowed down and worshipped at her shrine, yet beneath her corsets, I alone knew, there beat a heart from which, alas! all love and sympathy had long ago died out. To her, excitement, change, and flirtation were as food and drink; she could not live without them. Neither, indeed, could I, for, living with her ever since my convent days, I had imbibed her smart ideas and notions, stimulated by attacks of nerves.

A few days later, having lunched with Reggie and Gerald at the Grand Hotel, we went over to Monte Carlo by the two o'clock "yellow" express.

Reader, you probably know the panorama of the Riviera—that stretch of azure sky, azure sea, of golden coasts, purple hills fringed with olive and pine, rose and geranium running riot over hedge and hollow, oranges golden and flowers white upon the same branch. The pale violet of the Alps answers the violet of the valleys; white and gold marguerites spangle the hill-side where the old rock village of Eze is perched above; white and gold villas dot the wayside, and white and gold are the decoration of that Casino wherein is centred all the human vices—painted tastefully in white and gold—The Sign of the Seven Sins.

When I entered for the first time that wild, turbulent, close-smelling salle-de-jeu where the croupiers were crying in those mechanical, strident tones "Messieurs, faites vos jeux!" and uttering in warning voice "Rien ne va plus!" I gazed around me bewildered. Who were those grabbing crowds of smartly dressed people grouped around the tables? Were they actually civilized beings—beings who had loved, suffered, and lived, as I had loved, suffered, and lived?

How beautiful it was outside in that gay little Place with the red Hungarian band playing on the terrace of the Café de Paris, and half the grande monde of Europe lounging about and chattering. How enchanting was the grim Dog's Head as a fitting background in dark purple against the winter sunset, the old bronze Grimaldi rock rising sheer from the turquoise sea surmounted by the white tower of Monaco and the castellated walls of the Palace; to the right Villefranche and San Juan shining in topaz and amber,—the Esterels as a necklace of radiant jewels,—while to the left Bordighera was lying at the base of its neck, like a pearl at a fair throat. And beyond there was Italy—my own fair Italy! Out in that flower-scented, limpid air earth was a paradise; within those stifling gilt saloons, where the light of day was tempered by the thick curtains and the clink of gold mingled with the dull hum of the avaricious crowd, it was a veritable hell.

Some years ago—ah! now I am looking back: Ulrica is not at fault this time. No, I must not think. I have promised myself in writing this narrative not to think, but to try and forget all past unhappiness. Try. Ah! would that I could calm my soul—steep it in a draught of thoughtlessness, such that oblivion would come.

It is terrible to think how a woman can suffer and yet live. What a blessing it is that the world cannot read a woman's heart! Men may look upon our faces, but they cannot read the truth. Even though our hearts may be breaking we may wear a smile; we can fold our sorrows as a bird folds its wings, for they are part of our physical being; we can hide our grief so completely that none can know the burden upon us. Endurance, resistance, patience, suffering, all are, alas! a woman's heritage. Even in the few years I have lived I have had my share of them all.

I stood bewildered, watching the revolving red and black roulette-wheel and the eager crowd of faces around it.

"Vingt! Rouge, pair et passé!" the croupier cried, and a couple of louis which Ulrica had placed on the last dozen were swept away with the silver, notes, and gold to swell the bank.

I thought of my secret grief. I thought of Ernest Cameron and pursed my lips. The old Tuscan proverb which the nuns in Florence had taught me so long ago was very true, Amore non è senza amaro.

The millionaire's son at my elbow was explaining to me how the game was played, but I was paying no attention. I only remembered the man I had once loved—the man whose slave I was—the man whom I had forgiven, even though he had left me so cruelly.

Only three things could make life to me worth living—the sight of his face, the sound of his voice, the touch of his lips.

But they could never be, alas! we were parted for ever—for ever.

"Now, play this time," I heard Reggie beside me exclaim.

"Where?" I inquired mechanically, his voice awakening me to a sense of my surroundings.

"On the line, there—between the numbers 9 and 12."

I took a louis from my purse and with the rake carelessly pushed it upon the line he had indicated. Then I turned to talk with Gerald.

"Rien ne va plus!" cried the croupier.

A hundred necks were craned to watch the result.

The ball fell with a final click into one of the little spaces upon the wheel.

"Neuf! Rouge, impair et manque!"

"You've won, my dear!" cried Ulrica excitedly, and in a few moments Reggie, who raked up my winnings, gave me quite a handful of gold.

"There now," he said, laughing, "you've made your first coup. Try again."

I crammed the gold into my purse, but it would not hold it all. The three louis which would not go in I held in indecision in my hand.

"Play on the treize-dix-huit this time!" urged Reggie, and I obeyed him blindly.

The number 18 came up, therefore I again received another little handful of gold. I knew that many envious eyes were cast in my direction, and to me the excitement of winning was an entirely new sensation.

Ulrica fancied the last dozen, and I placed five louis upon it, winning a third time. Having won eight hundred francs in three turns of the wheel, I began to think roulette not such wearying fun as I had once believed it to be.

I wanted to continue playing, but the others prevented me. They knew too well that the bank at Monte Carlo only lends its money to the players.

With Reggie at my side I went out and strolled through those beautiful gardens beside the sea, watched the pigeon-shooting, and afterwards sat on the terrace of the Café de Paris and enjoyed the brilliant sundown.

CHAPTER III
IS A MYSTERY

I WAS LEFT ALONE with Reggie, for Ulrica had taken Gerald in to the orchestral concert.

"What awfully good luck you had!" he observed after we had been chatting some time. "If you'd had the maximum on each time you'd have won about four thousand dollars."

"There are a good many if's in gambling," I remarked. "I've never had any luck before in gambles at bazaars and such-like places."

"When you do have luck, follow it, is my motto," he laughed. "I should have advised you to continue playing today, only I thought it might annoy Ulrica," and he raised his glass to his lips.

"But I might have lost all that I won," I remarked. "No, I prefer to keep it. I'd like to be unique among the people and go away with some of the bank's money. I intend to keep what I have, and not to play again."

"Never?"

"Never!"

"My dear Miss Rosselli, that's what everyone says here," he laughed. "But before you've been on the Riviera long you'll discover that this is no place for good resolutions. Gambling is one of the sweetest and most insidious of vices, and has the additional attraction of being thought chic. Look at the crowd of women here! Why, every one of them play. If they didn't, others would believe them to be hard up—and poverty, you know, is distinctly bad form here. Even if a woman hasn't sufficient to pay her hotel bill she must wear the regulation gold chatelaine,—the gold chain-purse,—if it only contains a couple of pieces of a hundred sous. And she must play. Fortunes have been won with only five francs."

"Such stories, I fear, are only fairy tales," I said incredulously.

"No. At least one of them is not," he answered, blowing a cloud of smoke from his lips and looking at me amusedly. "I was playing here one night last March when a young French girl won three hundred thousand francs after having first lost all she had. She borrowed a five-franc piece from a friend and with it broke the bank. I was present at the table where it occurred. Fortune is very fickle here."

"So it seems," I said. "That is why I intend to keep what I've won."

"You might have a necklace made of the louis," he said. "Many women wear coins won at Monte Carlo attached to their bangles."

"A happy thought!" I exclaimed; "I'll have one put on my bangle tomorrow as a souvenir."

"Are you staying on the Riviera long?" he inquired presently.

"I really don't know. When Ulrica is tired of it, then we shall move down to Rome, I suppose."

"When she's lost sufficient, you mean," he smiled. "She's quite reckless when she commences. I remember her here several seasons ago. She lost very heavily. Luck was entirely against her."

I too remembered her visit. She left me in Washington and went to the Riviera for a couple of months, and on her return was constantly bewailing her penury. This, then, was the secret of it. She had never revealed to me the truth.

"And you think that I shall be stricken with the prevalent epidemic?" I inquired.

"I hope not," he answered quickly. "But after all, the temptation is utterly irresistible. It is sad, indeed, that here in this corner of God's earth, which He has marked as the nearest approach to paradise, should be allowed to flaunt all the vices and the seven deadly sins which render the world horrible. Monte Carlo is the one blot upon the Riviera. I'm a gambler,—I make no secret of it, because I find resistance impossible while I have money in my pocket,—nevertheless, much as I like a fling here each winter I would gladly welcome the closing of the Casino. It is, alas! true that those red-carpeted steps and the wide doors opposite form the entrance-gate to hell."

I sighed, glancing over to the flight of steps before us, where the gay wintering world in summer toilettes were passing up and down. He was possessed of common sense and spoke the truth. Inside those rooms the perspiring, perfumed crowds were fluttering around the tables as moths around a candle, going headlong to ruin both moral and financial.

"Yes," I observed reflectively, "I suppose you're right. Thousands have been ruined within that place."

"And thousands have ended by committing suicide," he added. "The average number of suicides within this tiny Principality of Monaco is more than two a day!"

"More than two a day!" I exclaimed incredulously.

"Yes. Of course, the authorities bribe the press and hush it all up, but the authentic figures were published not so long ago. The Administration of the Casino find it cheaper to bury a corpse than to pay a ruined gambler's fare to St. Petersburg, London, or New York. That's why the poor devils who are cleaned out find the much-talked-of viatique so difficult to obtain. Human life is held very cheap here, I can tell you."

"Oh, don't talk like that," I protested. "You make one feel quite nervous. Do you mean that murder is often committed?"

"Well—not exactly that. But one must always remember that here, mixing with the best people of Europe, are the very scum of the world, both male and female. Although they dress elegantly, live well, play boldly, and give themselves airs and titles of nobility, they are a very queer and unscrupulous crowd, I can assure you."

"Do you know any of them by sight?" I inquired, much interested.

"Oh, one or two," he answered, laughing indifferently. "Some of them, of course, are eccentric and quite harmless characters." Then a moment later he added: "Do you see that tall, thin old man just ascending the steps—the one with the soft, white felt hat? Well, his is a curious story. Twenty years ago he came here a millionaire, and within a month lost everything he possessed at trente-et-quarante. So huge were the profits made by the bank, that instead of giving him his viatique to London they allotted him a pension of a louis a day for life, on the understanding that he should never again enter the Rooms. For nearly twenty years he lived in Nice, haunting the Promenade des Anglais and brooding over his past foolishness. Last year, however, somebody unexpectedly died and left him quite comfortably off, whereupon he paid back to Monte Carlo all that he had received and returned again to gamble. His luck, however, has proved just as bad as before. Yet each month as soon as he draws his income he comes over, and in a single day flings it all away upon the red, his favorite color. His history is only one of many."

With interest I looked at the tall, thin-faced old gambler as he painfully ascended the steps, and even as I watched he passed in, eager to fling away all that stood between himself and starvation.

Truly the little world of Monte Carlo is a very queer place.

Ulrica and Gerald came laughing across the leafy Place and joined us at our table. It was very pleasant there, with the band playing the latest waltzes, the gay promenaders strolling beneath the palms, the bright flowers, and the pigeons strutting in the roadway. Indeed, as one sat there it seemed hard to believe that this was actually the much-talked-of Monte Carlo—the plague spot of Europe.

I don't think that I ever saw Ulrica look so well as on that afternoon in her white serge dress, which she had had made in Paris; for white serge is, as you know, de rigueur at Monte in winter, with a white hat and white shoes. I was also in white, but it never suits me as it does her; yet one must be smart, even at the expense of one's complexion. At Monte Carlo one must at least be respectable, even in one's vices.

"Come, let's go back to the Rooms," suggested Ulrica when she had finished her tea, flavored with orange-flower water, which is the mode at the Café de Paris.

"Miss Rosselli won't play any more," said Reggie.

"My dear Carmela," cried Ulrica; "why, surely you've the pluck to follow your good fortune?"

But I was obdurate, and although I accompanied the others I did not risk a single sou.

The place was crowded and the atmosphere absolutely unbearable, as it always becomes about five o'clock. The Administration appear afraid of letting in a little air to cool the heads of the players, hence the rooms are hermetically sealed.

As I wandered about with Reggie, he pointed out to me other well-known characters in the Rooms—the queer old fellow who carries a bag purse made of colored beads; the old hag with a mustache who always brings her own rake; the bright-eyed, dashing woman known to the croupiers as "The Golden Hand;" the thin, wizen-faced little hunchback who one night a few months before had broken the bank at the first roulette table on the left; men working so-called "systems" and women trying to snatch up other people's winnings. Now and then my companion placed a louis upon a transversale or colonne and once or twice he won, but, declaring that he had no luck that day, he soon grew as tired of it as myself.

Ulrica came up to us presently flushed with excitement. She had won three hundred francs at the table where she always played. Her favorite croupier was turning the wheel, and he always brought her luck. We both had won, and she declared it to be a happy augury for the future.

While we were standing there the croupier's voice sounded loud and clear "Zero!" with that long roll of the "r" which habitués of the Rooms know so well.

"Zero!" cried Reggie. "By Jove! I must put something on," and he dashed over to the table and handed the croupier a hundred-franc note, with a request to put it on the number 29.

The game was made and the ball fell.

"Vingt-neuf! Rouge, impair et passé!"

"By Jove!" cried Gerald, "he's won! Lucky devil! How extraordinary that after zero the number twenty-nine so invariably follows!"

The croupier handed Reggie three thousand-franc notes and quite a handful of gold. Then the lucky player moved his original stake on to the little square marked 36.

Again he won—and again and again. The three thousand-franc notes he had just received he placed upon the middle dozen. The number 18 turned up, and the croupier handed him six thousand francs—the maximum paid by the bank on a single coup. Every eye around that table watched him narrowly. People began to follow his play, placing their money beside his, and time after time he won, making only a few unimportant losses.

We stood watching him in silent wonder. The luck of the man with whom I had been flirting was simply marvellous. Sometimes he distributed his stakes on the color, the dozen, and the "pair," and in that manner often won in several places at the same coup. The eager, grabbing crowd surged around the table, and the excitement quickly rose to fever-heat. The assault Reggie was making upon the bank was certainly a formidable one. His inner pockets bulged with the handfuls of notes he crammed there, while the outer pockets of his jacket were heavy with golden louis.

Ulrica stood behind him, but uttered no word. To speak to a person while playing is believed by the gambler to bring evil fortune. When he could cram no more notes into his pockets he passed them to Ulrica, who held them in an overflow bundle in her hand.

He tossed a thousand francs on the red, but lost, together with the dozens of others who had followed his play.

He played again with no better result.

A third time he played on the red, which had not been up for nine times in succession, a most unusual run.

Black won.

"I've finished," he said, turning to us with a laugh. "Let's get out of this; my luck has changed."

"Marvellous!" cried Ulrica. "Why, you must have won quite a fortune."

"We'll go across to the Café and count it," he said, and we all walked out together. Then while sitting at one of the tables we assisted him to count the piles of gold and notes.

He had, we found, won over sixty thousand francs.

At his invitation we went along to Gast's, the jewellers in the Galerie, and he there purchased for each of us a ring as a little souvenir of the day. Afterwards we turned into Ciro's and dined.

Yes, life at Monte Carlo is absolutely intoxicating. Now, however, that I sit here reflecting on the events of that day when I first entered the Sign of the Seven Sins, I find that even though the display of such wealth as one sees upon the tables is dazzling, yet my first impression of it has never been altered. I hated Monte Carlo from the first—I hate it now.

The talk at dinner was, of course, the argot of the Rooms. At Monte Carlo the conversation is always of play. If you meet an acquaintance, you do not ask after her health, but of her luck and her latest successes.

The two bejewelled worlds, the monde and the demi-monde, ate, drank, and chattered in that restaurant of world-renown. The company was cosmopolitan, the conversation polyglot, the dishes marvellous. At the table next us there sat the Grand Duke Michael of Russia with his wife, and beyond a British Earl with a couple of smart military men. The United States Ambassador to Germany was at another table with a small party of friends, while La Juniori, Derval, and several other well-known Parisian beauties were scattered here and there.

I was laughing at a joke of Reggie's when suddenly I raised my eyes and saw a pair of new-comers. The man was tall, dark, handsome, with a face a trifle bronzed—a face I knew, alas! too well.

I started and must have turned pale, for I knew from Ulrica's expression that she noticed it.

The man who entered there, as though to taunt me with his presence, was Ernest Cameron, that man whom I had loved,—nay, whom I still loved,—the man who had a year ago cast me aside for another, and left me to wear out my young heart in sorrow and suffering.

That woman was with him—the tow-haired woman whom they told me he had promised to make his wife. I had never seen her before; she was rather petite, with a fair, fluffy coiffure, blue-gray eyes, and pink-and-white cheeks. She had earned, I afterwards heard, a rather unenviable notoriety in Paris on account of some scandal or other, but the real truth of it I could never ascertain.

Our eyes met as she entered, but she was unaware that she gazed upon the woman who was her rival and who hated her. She had stolen Ernest from me, and I felt that I could rise there, in that public place, and crush the life from her slim, fragile frame.

Ernest himself brushed past my chair, but without recognizing me, and went down the room gayly with his companion.

"Do you notice who has just entered?" asked Ulrica.

I nodded. I could not speak.

"Who?" inquired Reggie quickly.

"Some friends of ours," she answered carelessly.

"Oh, everyone meets friends here," he laughed, and swallowed his champagne unsuspectingly.

Reader, if you are a woman you will fully understand how sight of that man who held me in a fatal fascination caused within me a whirl of passions. I hated and loved at the same instant. Even though we were parted, I had never ceased to think of him. For me the world had no longer any charm, for the light of my life had now gone out, and I was suffering in silence, just as all women do who become the sport of fate.

Yes, Ulrica's notion was, after all, very true. No man whom I had ever met was really worth consideration. All were egoists. The rich believed that woman was a mere toy, while the poor were always ineligible.

Reggie spoke to me, but I scarcely heeded him. Now that the man I loved was near me I felt an increasing desire to get rid of this male encumbrance. True, he was rich, and I knew by my own feminine intuition that he admired me, but for him I entertained no spark of affection. Alas! that we always sigh for the unattainable.

For me, the remainder of the meal was a dismal function. I longed to get another glimpse of that dark, bronzed face, and of the tow-haired woman whom he had preferred to me, but they were evidently sitting at a table in the corner out of sight. Ulrica knew the truth, and took compassion upon me by hastening the dinner to its end. Then we went forth again into the cool, balmy night. The moon shone brightly and its reflection glittered in a long stream of silver brilliance upon the sea, the Place was gayly lit, and the white façade of the Casino with its great illuminated clock shone with lights of every hue.

Across to the Hermitage we strolled and took our coffee there. I laughed at Reggie's pockets bulging with notes, for, the banks being closed, he was compelled to carry his winnings about with him.

While we sat there, however, a brilliant idea occurred to him.

"Nearly all these notes are small," he said suddenly. "I'll go into the Rooms and exchange the gold and small notes for large ones. They'll be so much easier to carry."

"Ah!" cried Ulrica. "I never thought of that. Why, of course!"

"Very well," he answered, "I sha'n't be ten minutes."

"Don't be tempted to play again, old fellow," urged Gerald.

"No fear of that!" he laughed, and with a cigarette in his mouth strode away in the direction of the Casino.

We remained there gossiping for fully half-an-hour, yet he did not return. It was only a walk of a couple of minutes from the Hermitage to the Casino, therefore we concluded that he had met some friend and been detained, for he, like Gerald, came there each winter and knew quite a host of people. One makes a large circle of acquaintances on the Riviera, many interesting but the majority undesirable.

"I wonder where he's got to?" Gerald observed presently. "Surely he isn't such an idiot as to resume play."

"No. He's well enough aware that there's no luck after dinner," remarked Ulrica. "We might, however, I think, take a last turn through the Rooms and see whether he's there."

This suggestion was carried out, but although we searched every table we failed to discover him. Until ten o'clock we lounged about, then returned by the express to Nice.

That he should have left us in that abrupt manner was certainly curious, but as Gerald declared he was always erratic in his movements, and that his explanation in the morning would undoubtedly be found entirely satisfactory, we returned together to the hotel, where we wished our companion good-night and ascended in the elevator to our own sitting-room on the second floor.

My good fortune pleased me, but my heart was nevertheless overburdened with sorrow. Sight of Ernest had reopened the gaping wound which I had so strenuously striven to heal by the aid of lighter loves. I now thought only of him.

Ulrica, who was in front of me, gayly pushed open the door of our sitting-room and switched on the light, but ere she crossed the threshold she drew back quickly with a loud cry of horror and surprise.

In an instant I was at her side.

"Look!" she gasped, terrified, pointing to the opposite side of the room. "Look!"

The body of a man was lying face downward upon the carpet, half hidden by the round table in the centre of the room.

Together we dashed forward to his assistance and tried to raise him, but were unable. We succeeded, however, in turning him upon his side, and then his white, hard-set features became suddenly revealed.

"My God!" I cried, awe-stricken. "What has occurred? Why—it's Reggie!"

"Reggie!" shrieked Ulrica, kneeling quickly and placing her gloved hand eagerly upon his heart. "Reggie!—and he's dead!"

"Impossible!" I gasped, petrified at the hideous discovery.

"It is true!" she went on, her face white as that of the dead man before us. "Look! there's blood upon his lips. See! the chair over there is thrown down and broken. There has apparently been a fierce struggle."

Next instant a thought occurred to me, and bending I quickly searched his inner pockets. The bank-notes were not there!

Then the ghastly truth became entirely plain.

Reginald Thorne had been robbed and murdered.

CHAPTER IV
RELATES SOME ASTOUNDING FACTS

THE AMAZING DISCOVERY HELD us in speechless bewilderment.

The favorite of Fortune, who only a couple of hours before had been so full of life and buoyant spirits, and who had left us with a promise to return within ten minutes, was now lying still and dead in the privacy of our own room. The ghastly truth was so strange and unexpected as to utterly stagger belief. A mysterious and dastardly crime had evidently been committed there.

I scarce knew what occurred during the quarter of an hour that immediately followed our astounding discovery. All I remember is that Ulrica, with her face blanched to the lips, ran out into the corridor and raised the alarm. Then there arrived a crowd of waiters, chambermaids, and visitors, everyone excitedly asking strings of questions, until the hotel manager came and closed the door upon them all. The discovery caused the most profound sensation, especially when the police and doctor arrived, quickly followed by two detectives.

The doctor, a short, stout Frenchman, at once pronounced that poor Reggie had been dead more than half-an-hour, but the cursory examination he was enabled to make was insufficient to establish the cause of death.

"Do you incline to a theory of death through violence?" one of the detectives inquired.

"Ah! At present I cannot tell," the other answered dubiously. "It is not at all plain that m'sieur has been murdered."

Both Ulrica and I quickly found ourselves in a most unpleasant position. First, a man had been found dead in our apartments, which was sufficient to cause a good deal of ill-natured gossip; and secondly, the police seemed to entertain some suspicion of us. We were both cross-questioned separately as to Reggie's identity, what we knew of him, and of our doings at Monte Carlo that day. In response, we made no secret of our movements, for we felt that the police might be able to trace the culprit—if indeed Reggie had been actually murdered. The fact that he had won that sum and that he had left us in order to change the notes into larger ones seemed to puzzle the police. If robbery had been the object of the crime, the murderer would, they agreed, no doubt have committed the deed either in the train or on the street. Why, indeed, should the victim have entered our sitting-room at all?

That really seemed the principal problem. The whole of the circumstances formed a complete and most puzzling enigma, but his visit to our sitting-room was the most curious feature of all.

The thief, whoever he was,—for I inclined towards the theory of theft and murder,—had been enabled to effect his purpose swiftly and leave the hotel without detection. Another curious fact was that neither the concierge nor the elevator-lad recollected the dead man's return. Both agreed that he must have slipped in unobserved. And if so, why?

Having concluded the examinations of Ulrica and myself and my Italian maid, Felicita, who had returned from her evening out and knew nothing at all of the matter, the police made a most rigorous search in our rooms. We were present and had the dissatisfaction of watching our best gowns and other articles tumbled over and mauled by unclean hands. Not a corner was left unexamined, for when the French police make a search they at least do it thoroughly.

"Ah! What is this?" exclaimed one of the detectives, picking from the open fire-place in the sitting-room a crumpled piece of paper, which he smoothed out carefully.

In an instant we were all eager attention. I saw that it was a sheet of my own note-paper, and upon it in a man's handwriting was the commencement of a letter:

"My dear Miss Rosselli, I have——"

There it broke off short. There were no other words. The paper had been crushed and flung away, as though the writer, on mature thought, had resolved not to address me by letter. I had never seen Reggie's handwriting, but on comparison with some entries in a note-book found in his pocket the police pronounced it to be his.

What did he wish to tell me?

About an hour after midnight we sent up to the Villa Fabron for Gerald, who returned in the cab which conveyed our messenger.

When we told him the terrible truth he stood open-mouthed, rooted to the spot.

"Reggie dead!" he gasped. "Murdered!"

"Undoubtedly," answered Ulrica. "The mystery is inexplicable, but with your aid we must solve it."

"With my aid!" he cried. "I fear I cannot help you. I know nothing whatever about it."

"Of course not," I said. "But now tell us what is your theory? You were his best friend, and would therefore probably know if he had any enemy who desired to wreak revenge upon him."

"He hadn't a single enemy in the world, to my knowledge," Gerald answered. "The motive of the crime was robbery, without a doubt. Most probably he was followed from Monte Carlo by someone who watched his success at the tables. There are always some desperate characters among the crowd there."

"Do you think, then, that the murderer was actually watching us ever since the afternoon?" I inquired in alarm.

"I think it most probable," he responded. "At Monte Carlo there is a crowd of all sorts and conditions of outsiders. Many of them wouldn't hesitate to commit murder for the sum which poor Reggie had in his pockets."

"It's terrible!" ejaculated Ulrica.

"Yes," he sighed, whilst his face grew heavy and thoughtful. "This awful news has upset me quite as much as it has you. I have lost my best friend."

"I hope you will spare no effort to clear up the mystery," I said, for I had rather liked the poor boy ever since chance had first thrown us together in Washington, and on the renewal of our acquaintance a few days previously my estimate of his character and true worth had considerably improved. It was appalling that he should be thus struck down so swiftly and in a manner so strange.

"Of course, I shall at once do all I can," he declared. "I'll see the police and state all I know. If this had occurred in England or in America there might be a chance of tracing the culprit by the numbers on the bank-notes. In France, however, the numbers are never taken, and stolen notes cannot be recovered. However, rest assured, both of you, that I'll do my very best."

There was a tap at the door at that moment, and opening it, I was confronted by a tall, dark-bearded Frenchman, who explained that he was an agent of police.

To him Gerald related all he knew regarding poor Reggie's acquaintances and movements while on the Riviera, and afterwards in company with the detective he went to the rooms we had abandoned and there gazed for the last time upon the dead face of his friend.

This sudden tragic event had cast a gloom over both Ulrica and myself. We were both nervous and apprehensive, ever debating the mysterious reason which caused Reggie to enter our sitting-room in our absence. Surely he had some very strong motive, or he would not have returned straight there and commenced that mysterious letter of explanation.

As far as we could discern, his success at the tables in the afternoon had not intoxicated him, for although young, he was a practised, unemotional player, and to him gains and losses were alike—at least, he displayed no outward sign of satisfaction beyond a broad smile when his winning number was announced by the croupier. No, of the many theories put forward, that of Gerald seemed the most sound, namely, that he had been followed from Monte Carlo with evil intent.

The *Petit Niçois*, the *Eclaireur*, and the *Phare du Littoral* were next day full of "The Mystery of the Grand Hotel." In the article we were referred to as Mademoiselle Y. and Mademoiselle R., as is usual in French journalism, and certainly the comments made by the three organs in question were distinguished by undisguised suspicion and sorry sarcasm. The *Petit Niçois*, a journal which had on so many recent occasions given proof of its anti-English and anti-American tone, declared its disbelief of the story that the deceased had won the large sum stated, and concluded by urging the police of Nice to leave no stone unturned in its efforts to discover the murderer, which it added would probably be found within the hotel. This remark was certainly a pleasing reflection to cast upon us. It was as though the journal believed that one of us—or both—had conspired to murder him.

Gerald was furious, but we were powerless to protect ourselves against the cruel calumnies of such torchons.

The official inquiry, held next day after the post-mortem examination had been made, revealed absolutely nothing. Even the cause of death puzzled the doctors. There was a slight cut in the corner of the mouth, so small that it might have been accidentally caused while he had been eating, and beyond a slight scratch behind the left ear there was no abrasion of the skin—no wound of any kind. On the neck, however, were two strange marks, like the marks of a finger and a thumb, which pointed to strangulation, yet the medical examination failed to establish that as a fact. He died, it was declared, from some cause which could not be determined. It might, indeed, have been a natural death the doctors admitted, but the fact that the notes were missing pointed very clearly and conclusively to murder.

That same evening, as the winter sun was sinking behind the Esterels, we followed the dead man's remains to their resting-place in the English Cemetery up in the olive-groves of Caucade, perhaps one of the most beautiful and picturesque burial-places in all the world. Winter and summer it is always a blaze of bright flowers, and the view over the olive-clad slope and the calm Mediterranean beyond is one of the most charming in all the Riviera.

The American chaplain performed the last rites, and then we turned sorrowfully away and drove back to Nice silently, full of gloomy thoughts.

The puzzling incident had crushed all gayety from our hearts. I suggested that we should leave and go on to Mentone, but Ulrica declared that it was our duty to remain where we were and give the police what assistance we could in aiding them to solve the inscrutable mystery. Thus, the days which followed were days of sadness and melancholy. We ate in our own room to avoid the gaze of the curious, for all in Nice now knew the tragic story, and as we passed in and out of the hotel we overheard many whisperings.

As for myself, I had a double burden of sorrow. In those hours of deep thought and sadness I reflected that poor Reggie was a man who might per-haps have become my husband. I did not love him in the sense that the av-erage woman understands love. He was a sociable companion, clever, smart in dress and gait, and altogether one of those easy men of the world who appeal strongly to a woman of my own temperament. When I placed him in comparison with Ernest, however, I saw that I could never have actually entertained a real affection for him. I loved Ernest with a wild, passionate love, and all others were now, and would ever be, as naught to me. I cared not that he had forsaken me in favor of that ugly, tow-haired witch. I was his. I felt that I must at all hazards see him again.

I was sitting at the open window one afternoon, gazing moodily out upon the Square Massena, when Ulrica suddenly said:

"Curious that we've seen nothing further of Ernest. I suppose, however, you've forgotten him."

"Forgotten him!" I cried, starting up. "I shall never forget him—never!"

In that instant I seemed to see his dark, handsome face before me, as of old. It was in the golden blaze of a summer sunset. I heard his rich voice in my ears. I saw him pluck a sprig of jasmine, emblem of purity, and give it to me, at the same time whispering words of love and devotion. Ah, yes, he loved me then—he loved me.

I put up my hand to shut out the vision. I rose and staggered. Then I felt Ulrica's soft hand upon my waist.

"Carmela! Carmela!" she cried. "What's the matter? Tell me, dear!"

"You know," I answered hoarsely, "you know, Ulrica, that I love him!" My voice was choked within me, so deep was my distress. "And he is to marry—to marry that woman!"

"My dear, take my advice and forget him," she said lightly. "There are lots of other men whom you could love quite as well. Poor Reggie, for instance, might have filled his place in your heart. He was charming, poor fellow. Your Ernest treated you as he has done all women. Why make yourself miserable and wear out your heart regarding a past which it is quite unnecessary to recall? Live as I do, for the future, without mourning over what must ever be by-gones."

"Ah! that's all very well," I said sadly. "But I can't help it. That woman loves him—every woman loves him. You yourself admired him long ago."

"Certainly. I admire lots of men, but I have never committed the folly of loving a single one."

"Folly!" I cried angrily. "You call love folly?"

"Why, of course," she laughed. "Do dry your eyes, or you'll look an awful sight when Gerald comes. He said he would go for a walk with us on the Promenade at four, and it's already half-past three. Come, it's time we dressed."

I sighed heavily. Yes, it was true that Ulrica was utterly heartless towards those who admired her. I had with regret noticed her careless attitude times without number. She was a smart woman who thought only of her own good looks, her own toilettes, and her own amusements. Men amused her by their flattery, and she therefore tolerated them. She had told me so long ago with her own lips, and had urged me to follow her example.

"Ulrica," I said at last, "forgive me—forgive me; but I am so unhappy. Don't let us speak of him again. I will try to forget, indeed I will—I will try and regard him as dead. I forgot myself—forgive me, dear."

"Yes, forget him, there's a dear," she said, kissing me. "And now call Felicita and let us dress. Gerald hates to be kept waiting, you know."

CHAPTER V
DEALS WITH A MILLIONAIRE

ONE EVENING, ABOUT TEN days later, we dined at old Benjamin Keppel's invitation at the Villa Fabron.

Visitors to Nice know the great white mansion. High up above the sea, beyond the Magnam bridge, it stands in the midst of extensive grounds shaded by date-palms, olives, and oranges, approached by a fine eucalyptus avenue, and rendered bright with flowers, its dazzlingly white walls relieved by the green persiennes, a residence magnificent even for Nice, the town of princes. Along the whole front of the great place there runs a broad marble terrace, from which are obtained marvellous views of Nice on the left, the gilt-domed Jetée Promenade jutting out into the azure bay, the old château, Mont Boron, and the snow-capped Alps, while on the right lies the valley of the Var and that romantic chain of dark-purple mountains which lie far away beyond Cannes, a panorama almost as magnificent as that from the higher Corniche.

The interior was, we found, the acme of luxury and comfort. Everywhere was displayed the fact that its owner was wealthy, yet none on entering there would believe him to be so simple in tastes and curiously eccentric in manner. Each winter he came to Nice in his splendid steam-yacht, the Vispera, which was now anchored as usual in Villefranche harbor, and with his sister, a small, wizen-faced old lady, and Mr. Barnes, his secretary, he lived there from December until the end of April.

Ulrica had met him several times in New York, and he greeted us both very affably. He was, I found, a queer old fellow. Report had certainly not lied about him, and I could hardly believe that this absent-minded, rather ordinary-looking old gentleman with disordered gray hair and beard and dark, deep-set eyes was Gerald's father, the great Benjamin Keppel, of Pittsburg.

Dinner, even though a stately affair, was quite a pleasant function, for the old millionaire was most unassuming and affable. One of his eccentricities displayed itself in his dress. His dining-jacket was old and quite glossy about the back and elbows, he wore a paper collar, his white tie showed unmistakable signs of having done duty on at least a dozen previous occasions, and across his vest was suspended an albert, not of gold but of rusty steel. There had never been any pretence about Ben Keppel in his earlier days, as all the world knew, and there was certainly none in these days of his affluence. He had amassed his fabulous fortune by shrewdness and sheer hard work, and he despised the whole of that chattering little ring which calls itself Society.

Ere I had been an hour in this man's society I grew to like him for his honest plain-spokenness. He possessed none of that sarcastic arrogance which generally characterizes those whose fortunes are noteworthy, but in conversation spoke softly, with a carefully cultivated air of refinement. Not that he was refined in the least. He had gone to the States as an emigrant from a little village in Norfolk, and had succeeded by reason of several striking inventions in the manufacture of steel in amassing the third largest fortune in the United States.

He sat at the head of the table in his great dining-room, while Ulrica and myself sat on either hand. As a matter of course, our conversation turned upon the mysterious death of poor Reggie, and both of us gave him the exact version of the story.

"Most extraordinary!" he ejaculated. "Gerald has already explained the painful facts to me. There seems no doubt whatever that the poor fellow was murdered for the money. Yet to me the strangest part of the whole affair is why he should have left you so suddenly at the Hermitage. If he changed the money for large notes, as we may suppose he did, why didn't he return to you?"

"Because he must in the meantime have met someone," I suggested.

"That's just it," he said. "If the police could but discover the identity of the friend, then I feel convinced that all the remainder would be plain sailing."

"But, my dear guv'nor, the police hold the theory that he did not meet anyone until he arrived in Nice," Gerald observed.

"The police here are a confounded set of idiots," cried the old millionaire. "If it had occurred in New York or Chicago, or even in Pittsburg, they would have arrested the murderer long before this. Here, in France, there's too much confounded controle."

"I expect if the truth were known," observed Miss Keppel in her thin, squeaky voice, "the authorities of Monaco don't relish the idea that a man should be followed and murdered after successful play, and they won't help the Nice police at all."

"Most likely," her brother said. "The police of the Prince of Monaco are elegant blue-and-silver persons who look as though they would hesitate to capture a prisoner for fear of soiling their white kid gloves. But surely, Miss Rosselli," he added, turning to me, "the Nice police haven't let the affair drop, have they?"

"I cannot say," I responded; "the last I saw of any of the detectives was a week ago. The man who called upon me then admitted that no clue had so far been obtained."

"Then all I have to say is that it's a public scandal!" Benjamin Keppel cried angrily. "The authorities here entertain absolutely no regard for the personal safety of their visitors. It appears to me that in Nice year by year prices have increased until hotel charges have become unbearable, and people are being driven over the frontier to Bordighera and San Remo. During these past two years absolutely no regard has been paid by the Nice authorities to the comfort of the visitors who bring them their wherewithal to live!"

"The guv'nor's disgusted," laughed Gerald across to me. "He's taken like this sometimes."

"Yes, my boy, I am disgusted. All I want in winter is quiet, sunshine, and good air. That's what I come here for. And I can get all that at San Remo, for the air is better even than here."

"But it isn't so fashionable," I observed.

"To an old man like me it does not matter whether a place is fashionable or not, my dear Miss Rosselli," he said with a serious look. "I leave all that sort of thing to Gerald. He has his clubs, his horses, his fine friends, and all the rest of it. But all the people know Ben Keppel, of Pittsburg. Even if I belonged to the most swagger of the clubs and mixed in good society,—among lords and ladies of the aristocracy, I mean,—I'd still be the same. I couldn't alter myself as some of 'em try to and do."

We laughed. The old man was so blunt that one could not help admiring him. He had the reputation of being niggardly in certain matters, especially regarding Gerald's allowance, but, as Ulrica remarked, there were no doubt plenty of people who would be anxious to lend money to the millionaire's heir upon post-obits, so that after all it didn't much matter. If inclined to be economical in one or two directions, he certainly kept a remarkably good table, but although there were choice wines for us, he drank only water.

When, with Gerald, he joined us in the great drawing-room, he seated himself near me and suddenly said:

"I don't know, Miss Rosselli, whether you would like to remain here and gossip or whether you'd like to stroll round the place. You are a woman, and there may be something to interest you in it."

"I shall be delighted, I'm sure," I said, and together we went forth to wander about the great mansion which all the world on the Riviera knows as the home of the renowned Steel King.

He showed me his library, the boudoirs which were never occupied, the gallery of modern French paintings, the Indian tea-room, and the great conservatory, whence we walked out upon the terrace and looked down upon the lights of the gay winter city lying at our feet, and that flash of white brilliance which ever and anon shoots across the tranquil sea and marks the dangerous headland at Antibes.

The night was lovely—one of those dry, bright, perfect nights which occur so often on the Riviera in January. At sundown the air is always damp and treacherous, but when darkness falls it is no longer dangerous even to those with the most delicate constitutions.

"How beautiful!" I ejaculated, standing at his side and watching the great white moon slowly rising from the sea. "What a fairyland!"

"Yes. It is beautiful. The Riviera is, I believe, the fairest spot that God has created on this earth," and then he sighed as though world-weary.

Presently, when we had been chatting a few minutes, he suggested that we should re-enter the house, as he feared that I, being in décolleté, might catch a chill.

"I have a hobby," he said, "the only thing which prevents me from becoming absolutely melancholy. Would you care to see it?"

"Oh, do show it to me," I said, at once interested.

"Then come with me," he exclaimed, and led me through two long passages to a door which he unlocked with a tiny master-key upon his chain.

"This is my private domain," he laughed. "No one is allowed here, so you must consider yourself very privileged."

"That I certainly do," I responded, and as he entered he switched on the electric light, displaying to my astonished gaze a large place fitted up as a workshop with lathes, tools, wheels, straps, and all sorts of mechanical contrivances.

"This room is a secret," he said with a smile. "If the fine people who sometimes patronize me with visits thought that I actually worked here they'd be horrified."

"Then do you actually work?" I inquired, surprised.

"Certainly. Having nothing otherwise to occupy my time when I severed myself from the works, I took to turning. I was a turner by trade years ago, you know."

I looked at him in wonderment. People had said he was eccentric, and this was evidently one of his eccentricities. He had secretly established a great workshop within that princely mansion.

"Would you like to see how I can work?" he asked, noticing my look of wonder. "Well, watch—excuse me," and he threw off his jacket, and having raised a lever which set one of the lathes at work he seated himself at it, selected a piece of ivory, and placed it in position.

"Now," he laughed, looking towards me, "what shall I make you? Ah, I know, an object useful to all you ladies is a box for your powder-puff—eh?"

"You seem to be fully aware of feminine mysteries, Mr. Keppel," I laughed.

"Well, you see, I was married once," he answered. "But in those days my poor Mary didn't want face-powder, bless her!"

And at that instant his keen chisel cut deeply into the revolving ivory with a harsh, sawing sound that rendered further conversation impossible.

I stood behind watching him. His grand old head was bent keenly over his work as he hollowed out the box to the desired depth, carefully gauged it, finished it, and quickly turned the lid until it fitted with precision and exactness. Then he rubbed it down, polished it in several ways, and at last handed it to me complete, saying,—

"There is a little souvenir, Miss Rosselli, of your first visit to me."

"Thank you ever so much," I answered, taking it and examining it curiously. Truly he was a skilled workman, this man whose colossal wealth was remarkable even among the many millionaires in the United States.

"I ask only one favor," he said, as we passed out and he locked the door of his workshop behind us,—"that you will tell no one of my hobby—that I have returned to my own trade. For Gerald's sake I am compelled to keep up an appearance, and some of his friends would sneer if they knew that his father still worked and earned money in his odd moments."

"Do you earn money?" I inquired, amazed.

"Certainly. A firm in Bond Street, London, buy all my ivory work, only they are not, of course, aware that it comes from me. It wouldn't do, you know. My work, you see, provides me with a little pocket-money. It has done so ever since I left the factory," he added simply.

"I promise you, Mr. Keppel, that I'll tell no one if you wish it to remain a secret. I had no idea that you actually sold your turnings."

"You don't blame me, surely?" he said.

"Certainly not," I answered.

It seems, however, ludicrous that this multi-millionaire, with his great houses in New York and Pittsburg, his shooting-box in Scotland, his yacht, acknowledged to be one of the finest afloat, and his villa on the Riviera, should toil at turning in order to earn a pound or two a week as pocket-money.

"When I worked as a turner in England in the old days I earned sixteen shillings a week making butter and bread plates, wooden bowls, salad spoons, and such like, and I earn about the same today when I've paid for the ivory and the necessary things for the 'shop,'" he explained. Then he added: "You seem to think it strange, Miss Rosselli. If you place yourself for a moment in my position—that of a man without further aim or ambition—you will not be surprised that I have, after the lapse of nearly forty years, returned to the old trade to which I served my apprenticeship."

"I quite understand," I responded, "and I only admire you that you do not, like so many other rich men, lead a life of easy indolence."

"I can't do that," he said. "It isn't in me to be still. I must be at work, or I'm never happy. Only I have to be discreet for Gerald's sake," and the old millionaire smiled—rather sadly, I thought.

CHAPTER VI
PLACES ME IN A PREDICAMENT

DAY BY DAY FOR many days we went over to Monte Carlo, why, I can scarcely tell. All visitors to Nice drift there as if by the natural law of gravitation, and we were no exception. Even though our memories of the Sign of the Seven Sins were painful on account of poor Reggie's mysterious death, we nevertheless found distraction in the Rooms, the crowds, and the music. Sometimes Gerald would act as escort, and at other times we went alone after luncheon and risked a few louis on the tables with varying success. We met quite a host of people we knew, for the season was proceeding apace, and the nearness of the Carnival attracted our compatriots from all over Europe.

And as the days passed my eyes were ever watchful. Truth to tell, Monte Carlo had an attraction for me, not because of its picturesqueness or its play, but because I knew that in that gay, fevered little world there lived and moved the one man who held my future in his hands.

In the Rooms, in the "Paris," in the Place, and in the Gardens I searched for sight of him, but, alas! always in vain. I bought the various visitors' lists, but failed to discover his name as staying at any of the villas or hotels. Yet I knew he was there, for had I not seen him smile upon that woman who was my rival?

The papers continued to comment upon the mystery surrounding poor Reggie's tragic death, yet beyond a visit from the United States Consul, who obtained a statement from us regarding his friends in Philadelphia and took possession of certain effects found in his room, absolutely nothing fresh transpired.

It was early in February, that month when Nice puts on its annual air of gayety in preparation for the reign of the King of Folly; when the streets are bright with colored decorations, great stands are erected in the Place Massena, and the shops of the Avenue de la Gare are ablaze with carnival costumes in the two colors previously decided upon by the fêtes committee. Though Nice may be defective from a sanitary point of view and her authorities churlish towards foreign visitors, nevertheless, in early February it is certainly the gayest and most charming spot on the whole Riviera. The very streets are full of life and movement, sweet with the perfume of roses and violets and mimosa, and at a time when the rest of Europe is held frost-bound summer costumes and sunshades are the mode, while men wear their straw hats and flannels upon that finest of all sea-walks, the palm-planted Promenade des Anglais.

Poor Reggie's brother, a doctor in Chicago, had arrived to obtain a personal account of the mystery, which, of course, we gave. Gerald also conducted him to the grave in the English Cemetery, whereon he laid a beautiful wreath and gave orders for a handsome monument. Then, after remaining three days, he returned to Genoa and thence by the North German Lloyd to America.

We became, meanwhile, frequent guests at the Villa Fabron, dining there often, and being always received cordially by the old millionaire. The secretary, Barnes, appeared to me to rule the household, for he certainly placed himself more in evidence than his employer, and I could see that the relations between Gerald and this factotum of his father were somewhat strained. He was a round-faced man of about thirty-five, dark, clean-shaven, with a face that was quite boyish-looking, but with a pair of small eyes that I did not like. I always distrust people with small eyes.

From his manner, however, I gathered that he was a shrewd, hard-headed man of business, and even Gerald himself had to admit that he fulfilled the duties of his post admirably. Of course, I came into contact with him very little. Now and then we met on the Promenade or in the Quai St. Jean Baptiste, and he raised his hat in passing, or he would encounter us at the Villa when we visited there, but beyond that I had not spoken with him a dozen words.

"He has the face of a village idiot with eyes like a Scotland Yard detective," was Ulrica's terse summary of his appearance, and it was an admirable description.

On the Sunday afternoon when the first Battle of Confetti was fought we went forth in our satin dominoes of mauve and old gold—the colors of that year—and had glorious fun pelting all and sundry with paper confetti or whirling serpentines among the crowd in the Avenue de la Gare. Those who have been in Nice during Carnival know the wild gayety of that Sabbath, the procession of colossal cars and grotesque figures, the ear-splitting bands, the ridiculous costumes of the maskers, the careless, buoyant fun, and the good humor of everybody in that huge cosmopolitan crowd. Gerald was with us, as well as another young American named Fordyce, whom we had known at home and who was now staying at the Métropole over at Cannes. With our sacks containing the confetti slung over our shoulders and the hoods of our bright dominoes drawn over our heads and wearing half-masks of black velvet, we mixed with the gay crowd the whole of that afternoon, heartily participating in the fun.

I confess that I enjoyed, and shall always, I hope, enjoy, the Nice Carnival immensely. Many constant visitors condemn it as a tawdry tinsel show, and leave Nice for a fortnight in order to escape the uproar and boisterous fun, but after all, even though the air of recklessness would perchance shock some of the more puritanical in our own land, there is, nevertheless, an enormous amount of harmless, healthy fun to be derived from it. It is only soured spinsters and the gouty who really object to Carnival. The regular visitor to the Riviera condemns it merely because it is good form to condemn anything vulgar. They once enjoyed it, until its annual repetition became wearisome.

After the fight with confetti, during which our hair and dominoes got sadly tumbled, we struggled through the crowd to the hotel, and while Gerald went along to the café outside the Casino to wait for us we dressed.

Quite a host of people dined at the Villa Fabron that evening, including several pretty English girls. A millionaire never lacks friends. Old Benjamin Keppel was something of a recluse, and it was not often that he sent out so many invitations, but when he gave a dinner he spared no expense, and that in honor of Carnival was truly a gastronomic marvel. The table was decorated with mauve and old gold, the Carnival colors, and the room, draped with satin of the same shades, presented a mass of blended hues particularly striking.

The old millionaire headed the table, and in his breezy, open-hearted manner made everyone happy at once. Both Ulrica and I wore new frocks, which we considered were the latest triumphs of our Nice couturière,—they certainly ought to have been if they were not, for their cost was ruinous,—and there were also quite a number of bright dresses and good-looking men.

As I sat there amid the gay chatter of the table I looked at the spare, gray-bearded man at its head and fell into reflection. How strange it was that this man, worth more millions than he could count upon his fingers, actually toiled in secret each day at his lathe to earn a few shillings a week from an English firm as pocket-money. All his gay friends who sat around his table were ignorant of that fact. He only revealed it to those in whom he placed trust, and I was one of the latter.

After dinner we all went forth into the gardens, which were illuminated everywhere with colored lights and lanterns, wandering beneath the orange-trees, joking and chattering. A rather insipid young prig was at first my companion, but presently I found myself beside old Mr. Keppel, who walked at my side far down the hill until we came to the dark belt of olives which formed the boundary of his domain. Villas on the Riviera do not usually possess extensive grounds, but the Villa Fabron was an exception, for the gardens ran right down almost to that well-known white sea-road that leads along from Nice to the mouth of the Var.

"How charming!" I exclaimed, as, turning back, we gazed upon the long terrace hung with Japanese lanterns, and the moving figures, smoking, taking their coffee, and chattering.

"Yes," the old man laughed. "I have to be polite to them now and then, but after all, Miss Rosselli, they don't come here to visit me, only to spend a pleasant evening. Society expects me to entertain, so I have to. But I confess that I never feel at home among all these folks, as Gerald does."

"I fear you are becoming just a little world-weary," I said, smiling.

"Becoming! Why, I was tired of it all years ago," he answered, glancing at me with a serious expression in his deep-set eyes. It seemed as though he wished to confide in me, and yet dared not do so.

"Why not try a change?" I suggested. "You have the Vispera lying at Villefranche. Why not take a trip in her up the Mediterranean?"

"Would you like to go on a cruise in her?" he asked suddenly. "If you would, I should be very pleased to take you. I might invite a party for a run say to Naples and back."

"I should, of course, be delighted," I answered enthusiastically, for yachting was one of my favorite pastimes, and on board such a magnificent craft, one of the finest private vessels afloat, life would be most enjoyable.

"Very well, I'll see what I can arrange," he answered, and then we fell to discussing other things.

He smoked thoughtfully as he strolled beside me, his mind evidently much preoccupied. The stars were bright overhead, the night balmy and still, and the air was heavy with the scent of flowers. It was hard to believe that it was actually midwinter.

"I fear," he said at last,—"I fear, Miss Rosselli, that you find me a rather lonely man, don't you?"

"You have no reason to be lonely," I responded. "Surrounded by all these friends, your life might surely be very gay if you wished."

"Friends? Bah!" he cried in a tone of ridicule. "There's an attraction in money that is irresistible. These people here, all of them, bow down before the golden calf. Sometimes, Miss Rosselli, I have thought that there's no real honesty of purpose in the world."

"I'm afraid you are a bit of a cynic," I laughed.

"And if I am, may I not be forgiven?" he urged. "I can assure you I find life very dull indeed."

It was a strange confession, coming from the lips of such a man. If only I had a sixteenth part of his wealth I should, I reflected, be a very happy woman—unless the common saying were actually true, that great wealth only created unbearable burdens.

"You are not the only one who finds life wearisome," I observed frankly. "I also plead guilty to the indictment on frequent occasions."

"You!" he cried, halting and regarding me in surprise. "You—young, pretty, vivacious, with ever so many men in love with you? And you are tired of it all, tired of it while still in your twenties—impossible!"

CHAPTER VII
MAINLY CONCERNS THE OWL

ULRICA WAS THAT NIGHT wildly hilarious at my expense. She had noticed me walking tête-à-tête with old Mr. Keppel, and accused me of flirting with him.

Now, I may be given to harmless frivolities with men of my own age, but I certainly have never endeavored to attract those of maturer years. Elderly men may have admired me,—that I do not deny,—but assuredly that has been through no fault of my own. A woman's gowns are always an object of attention among the sterner sex. If, therefore, she dresses smartly, she can at once attract a certain section of males, even though her facial expression may be the reverse of prepossessing. Truth to tell, a woman's natural chic, her taste in dress, and her style of coiffure are by far the most important factors towards her well-being. The day of the healthful, buxom pink-and-white beauty is long past. The woman rendered artistic by soft chiffons, dainty blouses, and graceful tea-gowns reigns in her stead.

"Old Mr. Keppel walked with me because he wanted company, I suppose," I protested. "I had no idea such a misconstruction would be placed upon our conversation, Ulrica."

"Why, my dear, everyone noticed it and remarked about it! He neglected his guests and walked with you a whole hour in the garden. Whatever did you find to talk about all that long time?"

"Nothing," I responded simply. "He only took me round the place. I don't think he cares very much for the people he entertains, or he wouldn't have neglected them in that manner."

"No. But I heard some spiteful things said about yourself," Ulrica remarked.

"By whom?"

"By various people. They all said that you had been angling after the old man for a long time—that you had followed him to Nice, in fact."

"Oh Ulrica!" I cried indignantly. "How can they say such things? Why, you know that it was yourself who introduced us."

"I know," she answered rather curtly, "but I didn't expect that you would make such a fool of yourself as you have done tonight. Have you already forgotten Ernest?"

"Ah!" I cried, "you have no heart. Would that I had none. Love within me is not yet dead. Would to God it were. I might then be like you, cold and cynical, partaking of the pleasures of the world without a thought of its griefs. As I am, I must love. My love for that man is my very life. Without it I should die."

"No, no, my dear," she said quickly in a kindly tone, "don't cry, or your eyes will be a horrid sight tomorrow. I didn't mean anything, you know," and she drew down my head and kissed me tenderly on the brow.

I left and went to my room, but her words rang constantly in my ears. The idea that the old millionaire had been attracted by me was a novel one.

The whole theory was ridiculous. It had been started by some lying, ill-natured woman for want of something else to gossip about, therefore why should I heed it? I liked him, it was true, but I could never love him—never.

Reader, you may think it strange that we two young women were wandering about Europe together without any male relative. The truth is that that personage so peculiarly British, and known as Mrs. Grundy, is dead. It is primarily her complete downfall in this age of emancipation, bicycles, and bloomers that makes the modern spinster's lot in many respects an eminently attractive one.

We were discussing it over our coffee on the following morning, when Ulrica, referring to our conversation on the previous night, said,—

"Formerly, girls married in order to gain their social liberty; now, they more often remain single to bring about that desirable consummation."

"Certainly," I acquiesced. "If we are permitted by public opinion to go to college, to live alone, to travel, to have a profession, to belong to a club, to wear divided skirts,—not that I approve of them,—to give parties, to read and discuss whatsoever seems good to us, to go to theatres and even to Monte Carlo without masculine escort, then we have most of the privileges—and several others thrown in—for which the girl of twenty or thirty years ago was ready to sell herself to the first suitor who offered himself and the shelter of his name."

"I'm very glad, my dear, that at last you are becoming so very sensible," she answered approvingly. "Until now you have been far too romantic and too old-fashioned in your ideas. I really think that I shall convert you to my views of life in time—if you don't marry old Keppel."

"Kindly don't mention him again," I protested firmly. "To a certain extent I entirely agree with you regarding the emancipation of woman. A capable woman who has begun a career, and feels certain of advancement in it, is often as shy of entangling herself matrimonially as ambitious young men have ever shown themselves to be in like circumstances."

"Without doubt. The disadvantage of marriage to a woman with a profession is more obvious than to a man, and it is just the question of maternity, with all its duties and responsibilities, which is occasionally the cause of many women forswearing the privileges of the married state."

"Well, Ulrica," I said, "speak candidly, would you marry if you had a really good offer?"

"Marry? Certainly not!" she answered with a laugh, as though the idea was perfectly preposterous. "Why should I marry? I have had a host of offers, just as every woman with a little money always has. But why should I renounce my freedom? If I married, my husband would forbid this and forbid that—and you know I couldn't live without indulging in my little pet vices of smoking and gambling."

"Wouldn't your husband's love fill the void?" I queried.

"It would be but a poor substitute, I'm afraid. The most ardent love nowadays cools within six months, it seems, and more often even wanes with the honeymoon."

"I have really no patience with you," I said hastily; "you are far too cynical."

She smiled, sighing slightly. She looked so young in her pale pink peignoir.

"Contact with the world has, alas! made me what I am, my dear."

"Well," I said, "to be quite candid, I don't think that the real cause why so many women nowadays remain single is to be found in the theories we have been airing to one another. The fact is that after all we are only a bundle of nerves and emotions, and once our affections are involved we are capable of any heroism."

"You may be one of those, my dear," was her rather grave response. "I am afraid, however, that I am not."

I didn't pursue the subject further. She was kind and sympathetic in all else save where my love was concerned. My affection for Ernest was to her merely an amusing incident. She seemed unable to realize how terribly serious I was or what a crushing blow had fallen upon me when he had turned and forsaken me.

Gerald called at eleven, for he had arranged to accompany us over to the Farrells' at Beaulieu.

"Miss Rosselli," he cried as he greeted me, "you are a brick—that you are!"

"A brick!" I echoed. "Why?"

"Why, you've worked an absolute miracle with the guv'nor. Nobody else could persuade him to set foot on the Vispera except to return to New York, yet you've induced him to arrange for a cruise up the Mediterranean. What's more, we are going to leave that cur Barnes behind."

"Are you glad?" I asked.

"Glad! I should rather think so. We shall have a most glorious time! He intends asking the Farrells, Lord Eldersfield, Lord and Lady Stoneborough, and quite a lot of people. We've got you to thank for it. No power on earth would induce him to put to sea except yourself, Miss Rosselli."

The Carnival bal-masqué at the Casino, the great event of the King Carnival's reign, took place on the following Sunday night, and we made to a party to go to it. There were seven of us, and we looked a grotesque crowd as we assembled in the vestibule of the Grand attired in our fantastic garbs and wearing those mysterious masks of black velvet which so effectively concealed our features. Ulrica represented a Watteau shepherdess with wig and crook complete, while I was en bébé, a more simple costume surmounted by a sun-bonnet of colossal proportions. One of the women of the party was a Queen of Folly and another wore a striking Louis XV. dress, while Gerald represented a demon, and wore pins in his tail in order to prevent others pulling that dorsal appendage.

The distance from the hotel to the Casino is only a few hundred yards, therefore we walked, a merry, laughing group, for the novelty of the thing was sublime. Among our party only Gerald had witnessed a previous Carnival ball, and he had led us to expect a scene of wildest merriment.

Certainly we were not disappointed. Having run the gauntlet of a crowd who smothered us with confetti, we entered the great winter-garden of the Casino and found it a blaze of color—the two colors of Carnival. Suspended from the high glass roof were thousands of bannerets of mauve and old gold, while the costumes of the revellers were of the self-same shades. Everywhere were colored lights of similar hue, and the fun was already fast and furious. The side-rooms, which, as most readers will remember, are ordinarily devoted to gambling,—for gambling in a mild form is permitted at Nice,—were now turned into handsome supper-rooms, and in the winter-garden and the theatre beyond the scene was perhaps one of the liveliest and most animated in the whole world.

All had gone there to enjoy themselves. In the theatre there was wild dancing, the boxes were filled by the grand monde of Europe, princes and princesses, grand dukes and duchesses, counts and countesses, noted actresses from Paris and London, and well-known people of every nationality, all enjoying the scene of uproarious merry-making. We viewed it first from our own box, but at length someone suggested that we should descend and dance, an idea which was promptly acted upon.

Masked as every one was, with the little piece of black lace tacked to the bottom of the black velvet loup in order to conceal the lower part of the features, it was impossible to recognize a single person in that huge, whirling crowd. Therefore immediately we descended to the floor of the theatre we at once became separated from one another. I stood for a few minutes bewildered. The blaze of color made one's head reel. People in all sorts of droll costumes, false heads, and ugly masks were playing various kinds of childish antics. Out in the winter-garden clowns and devils were playing leap-frog and sylphs and angels, joining hands, were whirling round and round in huge rings playing some game and screaming with laughter. Almost every one carried miniature representations of Punch with bells attached, large rattles, or paper flowers, which when blown elongated to a ridiculous extent.

Never before in all my life had I been amid such a merry, irresponsible crowd. The ludicrousness of Carnival reaches its climax in the ball at the Casino, and whatever may be said of it, it is without doubt one of the annual sights of Europe. I have heard it denounced as a disgraceful exhibition by old ladies who have been compelled to admit that they had never been present, but I must say that from first to last, although the fun was absolutely unbridled, I saw nothing whatever to offend.

I was standing aside, watching the dancers, when suddenly a tall man dressed in a remarkable costume representing an owl approached, and bowing, said in rather good English, in a deep but not unmusical voice,—

"Might I have the pleasure of this dance with mademoiselle?"

I glanced at him in suspicion. He was a weird-looking creature in his bird dress of mauve and old gold and the strange mask with two black eyes peering out at me. Besides, it was not my habit to dance with strangers.

"Ah!" he laughed. "You hesitate because we have not been introduced. Here in Nice at Carnival one introduces one's self. Well, I have introduced myself, and now I ask you what is your opinion of my marvellous get-up. Don't you think me a really fine bird?"

"Certainly," I laughed. "You're absolutely hideous."

"Thanks for the compliment," he answered pleasantly. "To unmask is forbidden, or I would take off this terrible affair, for I confess I am half stifled. But if I'm ugly you are absolutely charming. It is a case of Beauty and the Bird. Aren't my wings fetching?"

"Very."

"I knew you were American. Funny how we Frenchmen can always spot Americans."

"How did you know that I was American?" I inquired.

"Ah! now that's a secret," he laughed. "But hark! it's a waltz. Come under my wing, and let's dance. I know you'd dearly love a turn round. For this once throw the introduction farce to the winds and let me take you round. The owl is never a ferocious bird, you know."

For a moment I hesitated, then, consenting, I whirled away among the dancers with my strange, unknown partner.

"I saw you up in that box," he said presently. "I waited for you to come down."

"Why?" With a woman's innate coquetry I felt a delight in misleading him, just as he was trying to mislead me. There was a decided air of adventure in that curious meeting. Besides, so many of the dresses were absolutely alike that now we had become separated it was impossible for me to discover any of our party. The Nice dressmakers make dozens of Carnival dresses exactly similar, and when the wearers are masked it is hard to distinguish one from the other.

"Well," he said evasively in answer to my question, "I wanted a partner."

"And so you waited for me? Surely any other would have done as well?"

"No, that is just it. They wouldn't. I wanted to dance with you."

The waltz had ended, and we strolled together out of the theatre into the great winter-garden with its bright flower-beds and graceful palms, a kind of huge conservatory which forms a gay promenade each evening in the season.

"I don't see why you should entertain such a desire," I said. "Besides," and I paused to gain breath for the little untruth, "I fear that my husband will be furious if he has noticed us."

"I might say the same about my wife—if I wished to import fiction into the romance," he said.

"Then you have no wife?" I suggested with a laugh.

"My wife is just as real as your husband," he responded bluntly.

"What do you mean?"

"I mean that if you really have a husband it is an extremely surprising confession."

"Why surprising?"

"Well, it's true that husbands are like Somebody's sewing-machines—no home being complete without one," he laughed. "But I really had no idea that Mademoiselle Carmela Rosselli possessed such a useful commodity."

"What!" I gasped, glaring at the hideous-looking Owl, "you know me?"

"Yes," he responded in a deeper voice, more earnestly than before. "I know quite well who you are. I have come here tonight expressly to speak with you."

I started, and stood glaring at him in wonderment.

"I have," he added in a low, confidential tone, "something important to say to you—something most important."

CHAPTER VIII
NARRATES A MYSTERIOUS INCIDENT

"YOU ARE A PERFECT stranger, sir," I said with considerable hauteur. "Until you care to give me your name, and make known who you are, I have no wish to hear this important statement of yours."

"No," he answered. "I regret very much that for certain reasons I am unfortunately unable to furnish my name. I am The Owl—that is sufficient."

"No, not for me. I am not in the habit of thus chattering with strangers at a public ball, therefore I wish you good-evening," I said, and turned abruptly away.

In an instant he was again by my side.

"Listen, Miss Rosselli," he said in a deeply earnest tone. "You must listen to me. I have something to tell you which closely concerns yourself—your future welfare."

"Well?" I inquired.

"I can't speak here, as someone may overhear. I had to exercise the greatest precaution in approaching you, for there are spies everywhere, and a single blunder will be fatal."

"What do you mean?" I inquired, at once interested. The manner of this hideously disguised man who spoke such excellent English was certainly mysterious, and I could not doubt that he was in real earnest.

"Let us walk over there and sit in that corner," he said, indicating a seat half hidden in the bamboos. "If there is no one near, I will explain. If we are watched, then we must contrive to find some other place."

"In our box," I suggested. "We can sit at the back in the alcove where no one can see us."

"Excellent!" he answered. "I never thought of that. But if any of your party should return there?"

"I can merely say that you invited me to dance, and I, in return, invited you there for a few moments' rest."

"Then let's go," he said, and a few minutes later we were sitting far back in the shadow of the box on the second tier, high above the music and gay revelry.

"Well?" I inquired eagerly when we were seated, "and why did you wish to see me tonight?"

"First, I have knowledge—which you will not, I think, deny—that you loved a man in Washington, one Ernest Cameron."

"Well?"

"And at this moment there is a second man who, although not your lover, is often in your thoughts. The man's name is Benjamin Keppel. Am I correct?"

"I really don't see by what right you submit me to this cross-examination upon affairs which are only my own," I responded in a hard voice, although I was puzzled to determine the identity of this masked man.

"Marriage with a millionaire is a temptation which few women can resist," he said philosophically in a voice undisturbed by my hard retort. "Temptations are the crises which test the strength of one's character. Whether a woman stands or falls at these crises depends very largely on what she is before the testing comes."

"And, pray, what concern have you in my intentions or actions?" I demanded.

"You will discover that in due time," he continued. "I know that to the world you, like your companion, Ulrica Yorke, pretend to be a woman who prefers her freedom and has no thought of love. Yet you are only acting the part of the free woman. At heart you love as intensely and hate as fiercely as all the others. Is not that so?"

"You speak remarkably plain, as though you were well acquainted with my private affairs," I remarked resentfully.

"I only say what I know to be the truth," he replied. "You, Carmela Rosselli, are not heartless, like that emotionless woman who is your friend. The truth is that you love—you still love—Ernest Cameron."

I rose in quick indignation.

"I refuse to hear you further, m'sieur," I cried. "Kindly let me pass."

His hand was on the door of the box, and he kept it there, notwithstanding my words.

"No," he said quite coolly. "You must hear me—indeed, you shall hear me!"

"I have heard you," I answered. "You have said sufficient."

"I have not concluded," he replied. "When I have done so you will, I think, only be anxious for me to proceed." And he added quite calmly: "If you will kindly be seated so as not to attract attention I will go on."

I sank back into my seat without further effort to arrest his words. The adventure was most extraordinary, and certainly his grotesque appearance held me puzzled.

"Here in Nice, not long ago," he continued, "you met a man who believed himself in love with you, yet a few nights later he was foully murdered in your sitting-room at the hotel."

"Reginald Thorne," I said quickly in a strained voice, for the memory of that distressing event was very painful.

"Yes, Reginald Thorne," he repeated in a low, hoarse voice.

"You knew him?" I asked.

"Yes, I knew him," was his response in a deep, strange tone. "It is to speak of him that I have sought you tonight."

"If you are so well aware of who I am, and of all my movements, you might surely have called upon me," I remarked dubiously.

"Ah! no. That would have been impossible; none must know that we have met."

"Why?"

"Because there are reasons—very strong reasons—why our meeting should be kept secret," the voice responded, the pair of sharp black eyes peering forth mysteriously from the two holes in the owl's sphinx-like face. "We are surrounded by spies. Here, in France, they have reduced espionage to a fine art."

"And yet the police have failed to discover the murderer of poor Mr. Thorne," I observed.

"They will never do that."

"Why not?"

"They will never solve the mystery without aid."

"Whose aid?"

"Mine."

"What?" I cried, starting quickly. "Are you actually in possession of some fact that will lead to the arrest of the culprit? Tell me quickly. Is it really certain that he was murdered, and did not die a natural death?"

"Ah," he laughed. "I told you a few minutes ago that you would be anxious to hear my statement. Was I not correct?"

"Of course. I had no idea that you were in possession of any fact or evidence regarding the crime. What do you know about it?"

"At present I am not at liberty to say—except that the person who committed the deed was no ordinary criminal."

"Then he was murdered, and the motive was robbery?"

"That was the police theory, but I can at once assure you that they were entirely mistaken. Theft was not the motive."

"But the money was stolen from his pockets?" I said.

"How do you prove that? He might have secreted it somewhere before the attack was made upon him."

"I feel certain that the money was stolen," I answered.

"Well, you are, of course, welcome to your own opinion," he answered carelessly. "I can only assure you that, even though the money was not found upon him, robbery was not the motive of the crime."

"And you have come to me in order to tell me that?" I said. "Perhaps you will explain further?"

"I come to you, Miss Rosselli, because a serious responsibility rests upon yourself."

"In what manner?"

"The unfortunate young man was attracted towards you; he accompanied you to Monte Carlo on the day of his death, and he was found dead in your sitting-room."

"I know," I said. "But why did he go there?"

"Because he, no doubt, wished to speak with you."

"At that late hour? I cannot conceive why he should want to speak with me. He might have come to me in the morning."

"No. The matter was pressing,—very pressing."

"Then if you know its nature, as you apparently do, perhaps you will tell me."

"I can say nothing," the deep voice responded. "I only desire to warn you."

"To warn me!" I cried, much surprised. "Of what?"

"Of a danger which threatens you."

"A danger? Explain it."

"Then kindly give me your undivided attention for a moment," the Owl said earnestly, at the same time peering into my eyes with that air of mystery which so puzzled me. "Perhaps it will not surprise you to know that in this matter of the death of Reginald Thorne there are several interests at stake, and the most searching secret inquiries have been made on behalf of the young man's friends by detectives sent from London and from New York. These inquiries have established one or two curious facts, but so far from elucidating the mystery, they have only tended to render it more inscrutable. As I have already said, the person actually responsible for the crime is no ordinary murderer, and notwithstanding the fact that some of the shrewdest and most experienced detectives have been at work, they can discover nothing. You follow me?"

"Perfectly."

"Then I will proceed further. Has it ever occurred to you that you might, if you so desired, become the wife of old Benjamin Keppel?"

"I really don't see what that has to do with the matter under discussion," I said with quick indignation.

"Then you admit that old Mr. Keppel is among your admirers?"

"I admit nothing," I responded. "I see no reason why you, a perfect stranger, should intrude upon my private affairs in this manner."

"The intrusion is for your own safety," he answered ambiguously.

"And what need I fear, pray? You spoke of some extraordinary warning, I believe."

"True, I wish to warn you," said the man in strange disguise. "I came here tonight at considerable risk to do so."

I hesitated. Then after a few moments' reflection I resolved upon making a bold shot.

"Those who speak of risk are invariably in fear," I said. "Your words betray that you have some connection with the crime."

I watched him narrowly, and saw him start perceptibly. Then I congratulated myself upon my shrewdness, and determined to fence with him further and endeavor to make him commit himself. I rather prided myself upon smart repartee, and many had told me that at times I shone as a brilliant conversationalist.

"Ah," he said hastily, "I think you mistake me, Miss Rosselli. I am acting in your interests entirely."

"If so, then surely you may give me your name, and tell me who you are."

"I prefer to remain unknown," he replied.

"Because you fear exposure."

"I fear no exposure," he protested. "I came here to speak with you secretly tonight because had I called openly at your hotel my visit would have aroused suspicion, and most probably have had the effect of thwarting the plans of those who are endeavoring to solve the enigma."

"But you give me no proof whatever of your bona-fides," I declared.

"Simply because I am unable. I merely come to give you warning."

"Of what?"

"Of the folly of flirtation."

I sprang to my feet indignantly.

"You insult me!" I cried. "I will bear it no longer. Please let me pass!"

"I shall not allow you to leave here until I have finished," he answered determinedly. "You think that I am not in earnest, but I tell you I am. Your whole future depends upon your acceptance of my suggestion."

"And what is your suggestion, pray?"

"That you should no longer regard old Mr. Keppel as your possible husband."

"I have never regarded him as such," I responded with a contemptuous laugh. "But supposing that I did,—supposing that he offered me marriage,—what then?"

"Then a disaster would fall upon you. It is of that disaster that I come here tonight to warn you," he said, speaking quickly in a hoarse, thick voice. "Recollect that you must never become his wife—never."

"If I did, what harm could possibly befall me?" I inquired eagerly, for the stranger's prophetic words were, to say the least, curious.

He was silent for a moment, then said slowly,—

"Remember the harm that befell Reginald Thorne."

"What?" I cried in alarm, "death?"

"Yes," he answered solemnly, "death."

I stood before him for a moment breathless.

"Then, to put it plainly," I said in an uneven voice, "I am threatened with death should I marry Benjamin Keppel."

"Even to become betrothed to him would be fatal," he answered.

"And by whom am I thus threatened?"

"That is a question I cannot answer. I am here merely to warn you, not to give explanations."

"But the person who takes such an extraordinary interest in my private affairs must have some motive for this threat."

"Of course."

"What is it?"

"How can I tell? It is not myself who is threatening you. I have only given you warning."

"There is a reason, then, why I should not marry Mr. Keppel?"

"There is even a reason why you should in future refuse to accept his invitations to the Villa Fabron," my strange companion replied. "You have been invited to form one of a party on board the Vispera, but for your personal safety I would presume to advise you not to go."

"I shall assuredly please myself," I replied. "These threats will certainly not deter me from acting just as I think proper. If I go upon a cruise with Mr. Keppel and his son I shall have no fear of my personal safety."

"Reginald Thorne was young and athletic. He had no fear. But he disobeyed a warning, and you know the result."

"Then you wish me to decline Mr. Keppel's invitation and remain in Nice?"

"I urge you for several reasons to decline his invitation, but I do not suggest that you should remain in Nice. I am the bearer of instructions to you. If you carry them out they will be distinctly to your benefit."

"What are they?"

"Today," he said, "is the eighteenth of February. Those who have your welfare at heart desire that you should, after the Riviera season is over, go to London, arriving there on the first of June next. You are familiar with London, of course?"

"Yes," I replied. This stranger seemed vastly well informed regarding my antecedents.

"Well, on arrival in London you will go to the Hotel Cecil and there receive a visitor on the following day, the second. You will then be given certain instructions which must be carried out."

"All this is very mysterious," I remarked. "But I really have no intention of going to London. By June I shall probably be in New York again."

"I think not," was his cold reply. "Because when you fully consider the whole circumstances you will keep the appointment in London and learn the truth."

"The truth regarding the death of Reginald Thorne?" I cried. "Cannot I learn it here?"

"No," he replied. "And, further, you will never learn it unless you take heed of the plain words I have spoken tonight."

"You tell me that any further friendship between Mr. Keppel and myself is forbidden," I exclaimed, laughing. "Why, the whole thing is really too absurd! I shall, of course, just please myself, as I always do."

"In that case disaster is inevitable," he observed with a sigh.

"You tell me that I am threatened with death if I disobey. That is certainly extremely comforting."

"You appear to regard what I have said very lightly, Miss Rosselli," said the unknown. "It would be well if you regarded your love for Ernest Cameron just as lightly."

"He has nothing whatever to do with this matter," I said quickly. "I am mistress of my own actions, and I refuse to be influenced by any threats uttered by a person who fears to reveal his identity."

"As you will," he replied with an impatient movement. "I am unknown to you, it is true, but I think I have shown an intimate knowledge of your private affairs."

"If, as you assure me, you are acting in my interests, you may surely tell me the truth regarding the mystery surrounding poor Reginald's death," I suggested.

"That is unfortunately not within my power," he responded. "I am in possession only of certain facts, and have risked much in coming here tonight and giving you warning."

"But how can my affairs affect anyone?" I queried. "What you have told me is, if true, most extraordinary."

"It is true, and it is, as you say, very extraordinary. Your friend Mr. Thorne died mysteriously. I only hope, Miss Rosselli, that you will not share the same fate."

I paused to look at the curious figure before me.

"In order to avoid doing so, then, I am to hold aloof from Mr. Keppel, remain in Europe until May, and then travel to London, there to meet some person unknown?"

"Exactly; but there is still one thing further. I am charged to offer for your acceptance a small present as some little recompense for the trouble you must be at in waiting here in the south and in journeying to London," and he drew from beneath his strangely grotesque dress a small box some four or five inches square wrapped in paper. This he held out to me.

I did not take it. There was something uncanny about it all.

"Do not hesitate, or we may be observed," he urged. "Take it quickly. Do not open it until you return to your hotel," and he thrust it into my hand.

"Remember what I have said," he exclaimed, rising quickly. "I must be gone, for I see that suspicion is aroused in those who are watching. Act with prudence, and the disaster against which I have warned you will not occur. Above all, keep the appointment in London on the second of June."

"But why?"

"Because for your own safety it is imperative," he responded, and with a low bow he opened the door of the box, and the next instant I was alone with the little packet the stranger had given me resting in my hand.

CHAPTER IX
SHOWS THE BIRD'S TALONS

FOR SOME LITTLE TIME after my mysterious companion had left I sat forward in the box, gazing down at the wild revelry below, and hoping that one or other of the party would recognize me.

So great a crowd was there, and so many dresses exactly similar, that to distinguish Ulrica or Gerald, or, indeed, any of the others, proved absolutely impossible. They might of course be in one or other of the supper-rooms, and I saw from the first that there was but little chance of finding them.

Leaning my elbows on the edge of the box, I gazed down upon the scene of reckless merriment, but my thoughts were full of the strange words uttered by the mysterious masker. The packet he had given me I had transferred to my pocket, and with pardonable curiosity I longed to open it and see what it contained.

The warning he had given me was extremely disconcerting and worried me. No woman likes to think that she has unknown enemies ready to take her life. Yet that was apparently my position.

That life could be taken swiftly and without detection I had plainly seen in the case of poor Reggie. When I recollected his terrible fate I shuddered. Yet this man had plainly given me to understand that the same fate awaited me if I did not adopt the line of conduct that he had laid down.

Whoever he might be, he certainly was acquainted with all my movements and knew intimately my feelings. There was certainly no likelihood of my marriage with old Benjamin Keppel. I scouted the idea. Yet he knew quite well that the old millionaire had become attracted by me and reposed in me a confidence that he did not extend to others. The more I reflected, the more I became convinced that the stranger's fear of being recognized arose from the fact that he himself was either the murderer or an accessory to the murder of poor Reggie.

What did the demand that I should return to London denote? It could only mean one thing—namely, that my assistance was required.

Whoever were my enemies, they were, I argued, enemies likewise of old Mr. Keppel. The present which the stranger had pressed upon me was nothing less than a bribe to secure either my silence or my services.

Try how I would, I could discover absolutely no motive whatever in it all. It was certain that this man, so cleverly disguised that I could not distinguish his real height, much less his form or features, had come there, watched for a favorable opportunity to speak with me, and then had warned me to sever my friendship with the millionaire.

Leaning there, gazing blankly down upon the crowd screaming with laughter at the Parisian quadrilles and antics of clown and columbine, I coolly analyzed my own feelings towards the blunt, plain-spoken old gentleman with the melancholy eyes. I found—as I had believed all along—that I admired him for his honest good-nature, his utter lack of anything approaching "side," his strenuous efforts to assist in good works, and his regard for appearances only for his son's sake. But I did not love him. No. I had loved one man. I could never love another—never in all my life.

Yet perhaps he was there disguised beneath a mask and dress of parti-colored satin! Perhaps he was down there among the dancers, escorting that woman who had usurped my place. The thought held me in wonder.

Suddenly I was brought back to a due sense of my surroundings by the opening of the door of the box and the entry of one of the theatre-attendants, who, addressing me in French, said:

"I beg m'zelle's pardon, but the Direction would esteem it a favor if m'zelle would step down to the bureau at once."

"What do they want with me?" I inquired quickly with considerable surprise.

"Of that I have no knowledge, m'zelle. I was merely told to ask you to go there without delay."

Therefore, in wonder, I rose and followed the man downstairs and through the crowd of revellers to the private office of the Direction, close to the main entrance of the Casino.

In the room I found the Director, an elderly man with short, stiff gray hair, sitting at a table, while near him stood two men dressed as pierrots, with their masks removed.

When the door was closed, the Director, courteously offering me a seat, apologized for disturbing me, but explained that he had done so at the request of his two companions.

"I may as well at once explain," said the elder of the two in French, "that we desire some information which you can furnish."

"Of what nature?" I inquired with considerable surprise.

"In the theatre, an hour ago, you were escorted by a masker wearing a dress representing an owl. You danced with him, but were afterwards lost in the crowd. Search was made through all the rooms for you, but you could not be found. Where have you been?"

"I have been sitting in the box in conversation with the stranger."

"All the time?"

"Yes, he took precautions against being seen."

"Who was he?"

"I have no idea," I responded, still puzzled at the man's demand.

"I had better perhaps explain at once to mademoiselle that we are agents of police," he said with a smile, "and that the movements of the individual who met you and chatted with you so affably are of the greatest interest to us."

"Then you know who he is?" I exclaimed quickly.

"Yes. We have discovered that."

"Who is he?"

"Unfortunately, it is not our habit to give details of any case on which we are engaged until it is completed."

"The case in question is the murder of Mr. Thorne at the Grand Hotel, is it not?"

"Mademoiselle guesses correctly. She was a friend of the unfortunate gentleman's if I mistake not?"

"Yes," I replied.

"Well," he said in a confidential tone, while his companion, a slightly younger man, stood by regarding me and tugging at his mustache, "we should esteem it a favor if you would kindly relate all that has transpired this evening. When we saw him meet you we were not certain of his identity. His disguise was puzzling. Afterwards there could be no doubt, but he had then disappeared."

"I had thought that the police had relinquished their inquiries," I said, nevertheless gratified to know that they were still on the alert.

"It is when we relax our efforts slightly that we have the better chance of success," the detective replied. "Did the man give you any name?"

"No, he refused to tell me who he was."

"And what was his excuse for accosting you and demanding a tête-à-tête?"

"He said he wished to warn me of an impending peril. In brief, he told me that my life was in jeopardy."

"Ah!" the man ejaculated, and exchanged a meaning glance with his companion. "And his pretence was to give you warning of it. Did he tell you by whom your life was threatened?"

"No. He refused any details, but he made certain suggestions as to the course I should pursue."

"That sounds interesting. What did he suggest?"

I hesitated for a few moments. Then, reflecting that the stranger was evidently under the observation of the police, and that the latter were still trying to bring poor Reggie's assassin to justice, I resolved to reveal all that had passed between us.

Therefore I gave a brief outline of our conversation, just as I have written it in the foregoing pages. Both detectives on hearing my story seemed very puzzled.

"You will pardon my intrusion," exclaimed the agent of police who had first spoken, "but as you will see, this is a clue which must be thoroughly investigated. Will mademoiselle forgive me for asking whether there is any truth in the man's surmise that you were about to become engaged to marry M'sieur Keppel?"

"None whatever," I answered frankly. "I can only suppose that some unfounded gossip has arisen, as it so often does, and that it has reached his ears."

"Yet he threatens—or at least warns you of peril—if you should become the wife of this wealthy m'sieur! Ah! there seems some very deep motive; but what it really is we must seek to discover. When we have found it we shall have, I feel confident, a clue to the murderer of M'sieur Thorne."

"But there is still another rather curious fact," I went on, now determined to conceal nothing. "He declared that it was necessary for my well-being that I should return to London, and there meet some person who would visit me on the second of next June."

"Ah! And you intend keeping that appointment, I presume."

"I intend to do nothing of the kind," I replied with a laugh. "The affair is a very ugly one, and I have no desire whatever that my name should be linked further with it."

"Of course. I quite understand the annoyance caused to mademoiselle. It is sufficient to have one's friend murdered in that unaccountable manner without being pestered by mysterious individuals who mask themselves and prophesy all sorts of unpleasant things if their orders are not obeyed. Did you promise to go to London?"

"I said I would consider the advisability of doing so."

"You were diplomatic—eh?" he said with a laugh. "It is unfortunate this fellow has slipped through our fingers so cleverly, very unfortunate."

"But if he is known to you there will surely not be much difficulty in rediscovering him?"

"Ah! that's just the question, you see. We are not absolutely certain as to his identity." Then after a slight pause he glanced at me and asked suddenly, "Mademoiselle has a friend—or had a friend—named Cameron—a M'sieur Ernest Cameron? Is that so?"

I think I must have blushed beneath the pieces of black velvet that hid my cheeks.

"That is correct," I stammered. "Why?"

"The reason is unimportant," he answered carelessly. "The fact is written in the papers concerning the case, and we like always to verify facts in such a case as this—that's all."

"But he has no connection with the tragic affair," I hastened to declare. "I haven't spoken to him for nearly two years—we have been apart for quite that time."

"Of course," said the man reassuringly. "The fact has nothing to do with the matter. I merely referred to it in order to gain confirmation of our information. You mentioned something of a proposed yachting cruise. What did this mysterious individual say regarding that?"

"He warned me not to go on board the Vispera——"

"The Vispera?" he interrupted. "The owner of the yacht is m'sieur the millionaire, is he not?"

I responded in the affirmative.

"And this M'sieur Keppel has invited you to go with others on a cruise to Naples?"

"Yes. But how did you know that it was to Naples?" I inquired.

"All yachts sailing from Nice eastward go to Naples," he answered, laughing. "I suppose the programme includes a run to the Greek islands, Constantinople, Smyrna, and Tunis—eh?"

"I think so, but I have not yet heard definitely."

"You have accepted the invitation, I take it?"

I nodded.

"And that, of course, lends color to the belief that m'sieur the millionaire is in love with you, for it is well known that although he has that magnificent yacht he never goes on a pleasure cruise."

"I can't help what may be thought by gossips," I said hastily. "Mr. Keppel is a friend of mine—nothing further."

"But this friendship has apparently caused certain apprehensions to arise in the minds of some persons of whom your mysterious companion was the mouthpiece—the people who threatened you with death should you disobey them."

"Who are those people, do you imagine?" I inquired, deeply in earnest, for the matter seemed to grow increasingly serious.

"Ah!" he answered with a shrug of his shoulders. "If we knew that we should have no difficulty in arresting the assassin of M'sieur Thorne."

"Well, what do you consider my best course?" I asked, utterly bewildered by the mysterious events of the evening.

"I should advise you to keep your own counsel and leave the inquiries to us," was the detective's rejoinder. "If this man again approaches you, make an appointment with him later and acquaint us with the time and place at once."

"But I don't anticipate that I shall see him again." Then, determined to render the police agents every assistance, even though they had been stupidly blind to allow the stranger to escape, I drew from my pocket the small packet which he had given me.

"This," I said, "he handed to me at the last instant, accompanied by a hope that I would not fail to keep the appointment in London."

"What is it?"

"I don't know."

"Will you permit us to open it?" he inquired, much interested.

"Certainly," I responded. "I am anxious to see what it contains."

The detective took it and cut the string with his pocket-knife; then, while his subordinate and the Director of the Casino craned their necks to investigate, he unwrapped paper after paper until he came to a square jewel-case covered in dark-crimson leather.

"An ornament, I suppose?" exclaimed the detective.

Then he opened the box, and from its velvet-lined depths something fell to the ground which caused us to utter a loud cry of surprise in chorus.

The detective bent and picked it up.

I stood dumfounded and aghast. In his hand was a bundle of folded French bank-notes—each for one thousand francs.

They were the notes stolen from Reginald Thorne by his assassin.

CHAPTER X
MAKES ONE POINT PLAIN

"Extraordinary!" ejaculated the detective, whose habitual coolness seemed utterly upset by the unexpected discovery. "This adds an entirely new feature to the case."

"What, I wonder, could have been the motive in giving the notes to mademoiselle?" queried his companion.

"How can we tell?" said the other. "It at least proves one thing, namely, that the man in the owl's dress is the individual we suspected."

"Do you then believe him to be the actual assassin?" I asked.

But the detectives, with the aid of the Director of the Casino, were busy counting the stolen notes. There were sixty, each for one thousand francs.

They examined the leather jewelry case, but found no mark upon it nor upon the paper wrappings. The box was such as might have once contained a bracelet, but the raised velvet-covered spring in the interior had been removed in order to admit of the introduction of the bank-notes, which, even when folded, formed a rather large packet.

"They are undoubtedly those stolen from M'sieur Thorne," the detective said. "In these circumstances it is our duty to take possession of them as evidence against the criminal. I shall lodge them with the Prefect of Police until we have completed the inquiry."

"Certainly," I answered. "I have no desire to keep them in my possession. The history connected with them is far too gruesome. But whatever motive could there be in handing them to me?"

"Ah, that we hope to discover later," the detective responded, carefully folding them, replacing them in the case, and taking charge of the wrappings, which it was believed might form some clue. "At present it would seem very much as though the assassin handed you the proceeds of his crime in order to convince you that robbery was not the motive."

"Then you do believe that the man in the owl's dress was the real culprit?" I cried eagerly. "If so, I have actually danced tonight with poor Reggie's murderer!" I gasped.

"It is more than likely that we shall be able to establish that fact," the subordinate observed in a rather uncertain tone.

"How unfortunate," ejaculated his superior, "that we allowed him to thus slip through our fingers—and with the money actually upon him too!"

"Yes," observed the Director of the Casino. "You have certainly tonight lost an excellent opportunity, messieurs. It is curious that neither of you noticed mademoiselle in the box talking with this mysterious individual."

"That was, I think, impossible," I remarked. "We sat quite back in the small alcove."

"What number was your box?" the Director asked.

"Fifteen."

"Ah! of course," he said quickly. "There is, I remember, a kind of alcove at the back. You sat in there."

"Well," observed the chief detective, "no good can be done by remaining here longer, I suppose, so we had better endeavor to trace this interesting person by other means. The fact that he has given up the proceeds of the crime is sufficient to show that he means to leave Nice. Therefore we must lose no time," and he glanced at his watch. "Ten minutes to two," he said. Then turning to his assistant, he ordered him to drive to the station and see whether the man who had worn the disguise of the night-bird was among the travellers leaving for Marseilles at two-thirty.

"Remain on duty at the station until I send and relieve you," he said. "There are several special trains to Cannes and Monte Carlo about three o'clock on account of the ball. Be careful to catch them all. It is my opinion that he may be going to cross the frontier at Ventimiglia. I'll telephone there as soon as I get down to the bureau."

"Bien, m'sieur," answered the other, and as they went out, wishing me good-night, I followed them, asking of the senior of the pair,—

"Tell me, m'sieur, what should be my best course of action. Do you think the threats are serious?"

"Not at all," he answered reassuringly. "My dear mademoiselle, don't distress yourself in the very least regarding what he has said. He has only endeavored to frighten you into rendering him assistance. Act just as you think proper. Your experience tonight has certainly been a strange one; but if I were in your place I would return to the hotel, sleep soundly, and forget it all until—well, until we make an arrest."

"You expect to do so, then?"

"We, of course, hope so. In my profession, you know, everything is uncertain. So much depends upon chance," and he smiled pleasantly.

"Then I presume you will communicate with me later as to the further result of your investigations?" I suggested.

"Most certainly. Mademoiselle shall be kept well informed of our operations, never fear."

We were at the door of the Casino, where a great crowd had assembled to watch the maskers emerging.

"Shall I call you a fiacre?" he asked quite gallantly.

"No, thank you," I responded. "I'll walk. It's only a few steps to the Grand."

"Ah, of course," he laughed. "I had forgotten. Bon soir, mademoiselle."

I wished him good-night, and next second he was lost in the crowd, while with my mind full of my extraordinary adventure I walked along the Quai St. Jean Baptiste to the hotel.

The incidents had been so strange that they seemed beyond belief.

I found the faithful Felicita dozing, but Ulrica had not returned. When she entered, however, a quarter of an hour later, she was in the highest of spirits, declaring that she had experienced a most delightful time.

"My opinion of the Carnival ball, my dear, is that it is by far the jolliest function on the Riviera," she declared. Then in the same breath she proceeded to give me an outline of her movements from the time we were lost to one another in the crowd. She had, it appeared, had supper with Gerald and several friends, and the fun had been fast and furious. Her dress was badly torn in places, and certainly her dishevelled appearance showed that she had entered thoroughly into the boisterous merriment of the Carnival.

"And you?" she inquired presently. "What in the world became of you? We searched everywhere before supper, but couldn't find you."

"I met a rather entertaining partner," I responded briefly.

"A stranger?"

"Yes," and I gave her a look by which she understood that I intended to say nothing before Felicita.

Therefore the subject was dropped, and as I resolved to tell her of my adventure later, she left me for the night.

I am seldom troubled by insomnia, but that night little sleep came to my eyes.

I lay there thinking it all over. I had now not the slightest doubt but that the man in the owl's dress was the assassin of poor Reggie. And I had chatted amicably with him. I had actually danced with him! The very thought held me horrified.

What marvellous self-confidence the fellow had displayed; what cool audacity, what unwarrantable interference in my private affairs, and what a terrible counter-stroke he had effected in presenting me with the actual notes filched from the dead man's pockets! The incident was rendered none the less bewildering on account of the entire absence of motive. I lay awake reflecting upon it the whole night long.

When we took our morning coffee together I related to Ulrica all that had passed. She sat, a pretty, dainty figure, in her lace-trimmed and beribboned robe-de-chambre, leaning her bare elbows upon the table, and listening open-mouthed.

"And the police actually allowed him to escape scot-free?" she cried indignantly.

"Yes."

"The thing is monstrous. I begin to think that their failure to trace the murderer is because they are in league with him. Here, abroad, one never knows. My dear Carmela, depend upon it that in this world of Monte Carlo the police are bribed just as the press, the railway men, and porters are bribed by those rulers of the Riviera, the Administration of the Société des Bains de Mer de Monaco."

"That may be so," I observed wonderingly. "But the fact still remains that last night I danced with Reggie's assassin."

"Did he dance well?"

"Oh Ulrica! Don't treat the thing humorously!" I protested.

"I'm not humorous. The worst of Carnival balls is that they're such mixed affairs. One meets millionaires and murderers, and rubs shoulders with the most notorious women in Europe. Your adventure, however, is absolutely unique. If it got into the papers what a nice little story it would make, wouldn't it?"

"For Heaven's sake, no!" I cried.

"Well, if you don't want it to reach the *Petit Niçois* or the *Eclaireur* you'd better be pretty close about it. Poor Reggie's murder is a mystery, and the public fondly delight to read anything about a mystery."

We discussed it for a long time, until the entrance of Felicita caused us to drop the subject. Yes, it was, as Ulrica had declared, an absolute enigma.

About four o'clock in the afternoon, when we had both dressed ready to go out,—for we had accepted an invitation to go on an excursion in automobile up to Tourette,—the waiter entered with a card, which Ulrica took and read.

"Oh," she sighed, "here's another detective! Don't let him keep us, dear. You know the Allens won't wait for us. They said four o'clock sharp, opposite Vogarde's."

"But we can't refuse to see him," I said.

"Of course not," she replied, and turning to the waiter ordered him to show the caller up.

"There are two gentlemen," he explained.

"Then show them both up," answered Ulrica. "Be sharp, please, as we are in a hurry."

"Yes, madame," responded the waiter, a young Swiss, and went below.

"I suppose they are the pair I saw last night," I said. "The police on the Continent seem always to hunt in couples. One never sees a single gendarme, either in France or Italy."

"One goes to keep the other cheerful, I believe," Ulrica remarked, and a few moments later the two callers were shown in.

They were not the same as I had seen in the Director's room at the Casino.

"I regret this intrusion," said the elder, a dark-bearded, rather unwholesome-looking individual with lank black hair. "I have, I believe, the honor of addressing Mademoiselle Rosselli?"

"That's me," I responded briefly, for I did not intend them to cause me to lose a most enjoyable trip in that most chic of latter-day conveyances, an automobile.

"We are police agents, as you have possibly seen from my card, and have called merely to ask whether you can identify either of these photographs," and he pulled forth two cabinet pictures from his pocket and handed them over to me.

One was a prison photograph of an elderly, sad-eyed convict, with baldish head and scraggy beard, while the other was a well-taken likeness of a foppishly dressed young man of about twenty-eight, the upward trend of his mustache giving him a foreign appearance.

Both were strangers to me. I had never seen either of them in the flesh, at least to my knowledge, and Ulrica was also agreed that she had never seen any one bearing the slightest resemblance to either.

"Mademoiselle is absolutely certain?" the detective asked of me.

"Absolutely," I responded.

"Will mademoiselle have the kindness to allow her memory to go back for one moment to the day of the unfortunate gentleman's death?" asked the detective with an amiable air. "At the time M'sieur Thorne was at the table at Monte Carlo and playing with success there were, I believe, many persons around him."

"Yes, a crowd."

"And near him, almost at his elbow, you did not see this man?" he inquired, indicating the bearded convict.

I shook my head.

"I really do not recollect any face of that excited crowd," I responded. "He may have been there, but I certainly did not see him."

"Nor did I," chimed in Ulrica.

"Then I much regret troubling you," he said, bowing politely. "In this affair we are, as you of course know, making very searching inquiries on account of representations made by the Ambassador of the United States in Paris. We intend, if possible, to solve the mystery."

"And the man who accosted me at the ball last night," I said. "Do you suspect him to be the original of that photograph?"

"At the ball last night? I do not follow mademoiselle."

"But I made a statement of the whole facts to two agents of your department at an early hour this morning, before I left the Casino."

He looked puzzled, and his dark face broadened into a smile.

"Pardon. But I think mademoiselle must be under some misapprehension. What occurred at the ball? Anything to arouse your suspicion?"

"To arouse my suspicion?" I echoed. "Why, a man attired in the garb of an owl accosted me, gave me a strange warning, and actually placed in my hands the sixty thousand francs in notes stolen from the dead man!"

"Impossible!" gasped the detective, amazed. "Where are the notes? You should have given us information instantly."

"I handed the notes to two police agents who were waiting in the Director's room, and to whom I made a statement of the whole affair."

"What!" he cried loudly. "You have parted with the money?"

"Certainly."

"Then mademoiselle has been most cleverly tricked, for the men to whom you handed the proceeds of the robbery were certainly not agents of the police!—they were impostors!"

CHAPTER XI
DESCRIBES A MEETING AND ITS SEQUEL

HIS WORDS STAGGERED ME.

"Not agents of police!" I cried, dumfounded. "Why, they were fully cognizant of every detail of the affair. It was the Director of the Casino who presented them."

"Then M'sieur the Directeur was tricked, just as you were," he answered gravely. "You say that you actually received from the hands of some one who wore an effective disguise the sum stolen from the unfortunate m'sieur? Kindly explain the whole circumstances of your meeting, and what passed between you."

"My dear Carmela," exclaimed Ulrica. "This fresh complication is absolutely bewildering. You not only danced and chatted with the murderer, but you were the victim of a very clever plot."

"That is quite certain," observed the officer. "The two individuals to whom mademoiselle inadvertently gave the notes upon the representations that they were agents of the police, were evidently well acquainted with the murderer's intention to give up the proceeds of the robbery, and had watched you narrowly all through the evening. But kindly give us exact details."

In obedience to his demand, I recounted the whole story. It seemed to me incredible that the two men who had sent for me were bogus detectives, yet such was the actual fact, as was shown later when the Director of the Casino explained how they had come to him, telling him that they were police agents from Marseilles, and had ordered him to send for me, as they wished to interrogate me regarding "the affair of the Grand Hotel." Such, he declared, was their air of authority that he never for a moment doubted that they were genuine officers of police.

My statement held the two men absolutely speechless. I told them of the strange appointment in London made by the man with the owl's face, of the curious warning he had given me, and of the manner in which he had presented me with the sum won at the tables by the murdered man.

"You can give us absolutely no idea whatever of his personal appearance?" he inquired dubiously.

"None whatever," I answered. "The dress and mask were effectual in disguising him."

"And the two men who falsely passed as police agents—will you kindly describe them?" And he took out a well-worn pocket-book and scribbled in it.

I described their personal appearance as closely as I could, while on his part he took down my statement very carefully.

"This is most extraordinary!" Ulrica observed, standing near me in wonder. "The pair who said they were detectives were exceedingly clever, and are evidently aware of all that has transpired."

"Marvellous!" exclaimed the man reflectively. "Only a very clever thief would dare to walk into the bureau of the Casino and act as they did."

"Have they any connection with the actual assassin, do you think?"

"I'm inclined to believe so," he responded. "It was a conspiracy on their part to obtain possession of the money."

"Of course, I gave it up in entire innocence," I said. "I never dreamed that such a plot could exist."

"Ah, mademoiselle," observed the detective, "in this affair we have evidently to deal with those who have brought crime to a fine art. There seems something remarkable regarding the appointment in London on the second of June. It seems as though it were devised to gain time with some secret object or another."

"I am absolutely bewildered," I admitted. "My position in this tragic affair is anything but enviable."

"Most certainly. All this must be most annoying and distressing to mademoiselle. I only hope we shall be successful in tracing the real perpetrators of the crime."

"You think there was more than one?"

"That is most probable," he replied. "At present, however, we still remain without any tangible clue, save that the proceeds of the crime have passed from one person to another through the agency of yourself."

"Their audacity was beyond comprehension!" I cried. "It really seems inconceivable that I should have danced with the actual murderer, and afterwards been induced to hand over to a pair of impostors the money stolen from the unfortunate young man. I feel that I am to blame for my shortsightedness."

"Not at all, mademoiselle, not at all," declared the detective with his suave Gallic politeness. "With such a set of ingenious malefactors it is easy to commit an error and fall a victim."

"And what can be done?"

"We can only continue our investigations."

"But the man in the owl's dress? Tell me candidly, do you really believe that he was the actual murderer?"

"He may have been. It was evident that for some hidden reason he had some strong motive in passing the stolen notes into your possession."

"But why?"

"Ah! that is one of the mysteries which we must try and solve. The man was French, you say?"

"He spoke English admirably."

"No word of French?"

"Not a single word. Yet he possessed an accent rather unusual."

"He might have been a foreigner—an Italian or German—for aught you know?" the detective suggested.

"No," I answered reflectively. "His gestures were French. I believe that he was actually French."

"And the bogus police agents?"

"They too were French, undoubtedly. It would have been impossible to deceive the Director of the Casino, himself a Frenchman."

"Mademoiselle is quite right. I will at once see M'sieur le Directeur and hear his statement. It is best," he added, "that the matter should remain a profound secret. Do not mention it, either of you, even to your nearest friends. Publicity might very probably render futile all our inquiries."

"I understand," I said.

"And mademoiselle will say no word to any one about it?"

I glanced at Ulrica inquiringly.

"Certainly," she answered. "If m'sieur wishes the affair shall be kept secret."

Then, after some further discussion, the police officer thanked us, gave us an assurance of his most profound respect, and, accompanied by his silent subordinate, withdrew.

"After all," I remarked when they had gone, "it will be best, perhaps, to say nothing whatever to Gerald. He might mention it incautiously, and thus it might get into the papers."

"Yes, my dear," answered Ulrica, "perhaps silence is best. But the trick played upon you passes comprehension. I don't like the aspect of affairs at all, and if it were not for the fact that we have so many friends here in Nice, and that it is just the centre of the season, I should suggest the packing of our trunks."

"We shall leave soon," I said, "as soon as the yachting party is complete."

That same night after our trip to Tourette we accompanied the Allens, a middle-aged American and his wife, who lived in Paris, over to Monte Carlo. The Battle of Flowers had taken place there during the day, and that event always marks the zenith of the gaming season. The Rooms were crowded, and the dresses, always magnificent at night, were more daring than ever. Half of fashionable Europe seemed there, including an English Royal Highness and a crowd of notables. One of De Lara's operas was being played in the Casino theatre, and his works, being great favorites there, always attract a full house.

The display of jewels at the tables was that night the most dazzling I had ever seen. Some women, mostly gay Parisiennes or arrogant Russians, seemed literally covered with diamonds, and as they stood around one risking their louis or five-franc pieces, it seemed strange that with jewels of that worth upon them they should descend to play with such paltry stakes. But many women at Monte Carlo play merely because it is the correct thing so to do, and very often are careless of either loss or gain.

The usual characters were there: the wizened old man with his capacious purse; the old hag in black cashmere and rouged face playing and winning; and, alas! the foolish young man who staked always in the wrong place until he had flung away his last louis. In all the world there is no stranger panorama of life than that presented at ten o'clock at night at the tables of Monte Carlo. It is unique, indescribable—appalling.

Temptation is spread before the unwary in all its forms, until the fevered atmosphere of gold and avarice throbs with evil, becomes nauseous, and one longs for a breath of the fresh night air and a refreshing drink to take the bad taste out of one's mouth.

I played, merely because Ulrica and Dolly Allen played. I think I won three or four louis, but am not certain of the amount. You ask why?

Because seated at the table exactly opposite to where I stood unnoticed among the crowd was Ernest Cameron.

At his side was the inevitable red and black card whereon he registered each number as it came up; before him were several little piles of louis and a few notes; while behind him, leaning now and then over his chair and whispering, was *that woman*!

At frequent intervals he played, generally upon the dozens, and even then rather uncertainly. But he often lost. Once or twice he played with fairly large stakes upon a chance that appeared practically certain; but he had no luck, and the croupier raked them in.

For fully a dozen times he staked two louis on the last twelve numbers, but with that perversity which sometimes seems to seize the roulette-ball, the numbers came up between 1 and 24.

Suddenly the tow-haired woman who had replaced me in his affections leaned over and said in a voice quite audible to me,—

"Put the maximum on number 6!"

With blind obedience he counted out the sum sufficient to win the maximum of six thousand francs, and pushed it upon the number she had named.

"Rien ne va plus!" cried the croupier next instant, and there, sure enough, I saw the ball drop into the number the witch had prophesied.

The croupier counted the stake quickly, and pushed with his rake towards the fortunate player notes for six thousand francs, folded in half, with the simple words,—

"En plein."

"Enough!" cried the woman prompting him. "Play no more tonight!"

He sighed, and with a strange, preoccupied air, gathered up his coin, notes, and other belongings, while a player tossed over a five-franc piece to "mark" his place, or, in other words, to secure his chair when he vacated it. Then, still obedient to her, he rose with a faint smile upon his lips.

As he did so, he raised his eyes, and they fell full upon mine, for I was standing there watching him.

Our gaze met suddenly. Next instant, however, the light died out from his countenance, and he stood glaring at me as though I were an apparition. His mouth was slightly opened, his hand trembled, his brows contracted, and his face grew ashen.

His attitude was as though he were cowed by my presence. He remembered our last meeting.

In a moment, however, he recovered his self-possession, turned his back upon me, and strolled away beside that woman who had usurped my place.

CHAPTER XII
CARRIES ME ON BOARD THE VISPERA

FACES, EVEN EXPRESSIONS, MAY lie, but eyes lie never.

A man may commit follies; but once cured, those follies expand his nature. With a woman, alas! follies are always debasing. It was, I knew, a folly to love him.

Life is always disappointing. The shattering of our idols, the revelation of the shallowness of friendship, the losing faith in those we love, and the witnessing of their fall from that pedestal whereon we placed them in our own exalted idealization—all is disappointing.

I stood gazing after him as he strode down the great room with its bejewelled, excited crowd, where the chevalier d'industrie and the declassé woman jostled with the pickpocket, the professional thief, and the men who gamble at Aix, Ostend, Namur, or Spa as the seasons come and go, that strange assembly of courteous Italians, bearded Russians, well-groomed Englishmen, and women painted, powdered, and perfumed; those reckless beings qui péchent à froid, who sin not through the senses but through indifference.

I held my breath; my heart beat so violently that I could hear it above the babel of voices about me. I suffered the most acute agony. Of late I had been always thinking of him—asleep, dreaming—always dreaming of him. Always the same pang of regret was within my heart, regret that I had allowed him to go away without a word, without telling him how madly, despairingly, I loved him.

Life without him was a hopeless blank, yet it was all through my vanity, my wretched pride, my invincible self-love. I was now careless, indifferent, inconsequential, my only thought being of him. His coldness, his disdain, was killing me. Yes, when his eyes had met mine in surprise, they were strange, Sphinx-like, and mysterious.

Yet at that moment I did not care what he might say to me. I only wished to hear him speaking to me: to hear the sound of his voice and to know that he cared enough for me to treat me as a human being.

Ah, I trembled when I realized how madly I loved him, and how fierce was my hatred of that woman who issued her orders and whom he obeyed.

I turned away with the Allens, while Ulrica cried delightedly that she had won on 16, her favorite number. But I did not answer. My heart had grown sick, and I went forth into the bright night air and down the steps towards the "ascenseurs."

On the steps a well-dressed young Frenchman was lounging, and as I passed down I heard him humming to himself that gay, catchy chanson so popular at the café concert:

> "*A bas la romance et l'idylle,*
> *Les oiseaux, la forêt, le buisson,*
> *Des marlous, de la grande ville,*
> *Nous allons chanter la chanson!*
> *V'la les dos, viv'nt les dos!*
> *C'est les dos, les gros,*
> *Les beaux,*
> *A nous les marmites!*
> *Grandes ou petites;*
> *V'la les dos, viv'nt les dos;*
> *C'est les dos, les gros,*
> *Les beaux,*
> *A nous les marmit' et vivent les dos!*"

I closed my ears to shut out the sound of those words. I remembered Ernest—that look in his eyes, that scorn in his face, that disdain in his bearing.

The truth was, alas! too plain. His love for me was dead. I was the most wretched of women, of all God's creatures.

I prayed that I might regard him—that I might regard the world—with indifference, and yet I was sufficiently acquainted with the world and its ways to know that to a woman the word indifference is the most evil word in the language, that it is the most fatal of all sentiments, the most deadly of all attitudes.

But Ernest, the man whose slave I was, despised me. He commanded my love. Why could not I command his? Ah! because I was a woman, and my face had ceased to interest him!

Bitter tears sprang to my eyes, but I managed to preserve my self-control and enter the station-lift making an inward vow that never again in my whole life would I set foot in that hated hell within a paradise called Monte Carlo.

True, I was a woman who amused myself wherever amusement could be obtained, but I still remained, as I had always been from those sweet well-re-

membered days at the gray old convent in Florence, an honest woman. At
Monte Carlo the scum of the earth enjoy the flowers of the earth. I detested
its crowds; I held in abhorrence that wild, turbulent avarice, and felt stifled in
that atmosphere of gilded sin. No. I would never enter there again. The bitter
remembrance of that night would, I knew, be too painful.

I returned to Nice with a feeling that for me, now that Ernest had drifted
from me to become a placid gambler and was indifferent, life had no further
charm. The recollection of the days that followed can never be torn from my
memory, my brain, my soul. I smiled, though I was wearing out my heart; I
laughed even though bitter tears were ready to start to my eyes, and I made
pretence of being interested in things to which I was at heart supremely indifferent. I courted forgetfulness, but the oblivion of my love would not come.
I never knew till then how great was the passion a woman could conceive for
a man, or how his memory could ever arise, a ghost from the past to terrify
the present.

That night as we drove from the station to the hotel Ulrica accidentally
touched my hand.

"How cold you are, dear!" she cried in surprise.

"Yes," I answered, shivering.

I was cold; it was the truth. At thought of the man who had forsaken me an
icy chill had struck my heart—the chill of unsatisfied love, of desolation, of
blank, unutterable despair.

In due course our yachting gowns came home from the dressmaker's,—accompanied by terrifying bills, of course,—and a few days later we sailed out
of Villefranche harbor on board the Vispera. The party was a well-chosen one,
consisting mostly of youngish people, several of whom we knew quite well,
and ere the second day was over we had all settled down to the usual routine
of life on board a yacht. There was no sensation of being cramped up, but,
on the contrary, the decks were broad and spacious, and the cabins perfect
nests of luxury. The vessel had been built on the Clyde according to its owner's
designs, and it certainly was a miniature Atlantic liner.

Our plans had been slightly altered, for as the majority of the guests had
never been to Algiers it was resolved to make a run over there and then coast
along Algeria and Tunis and so on to Alexandria. As we steamed away from
Villefranche the receding panorama of the Littoral, with its olive-covered
slopes and great, purple, snow-capped Alps, spread out before us, presenting
a perfectly enchanting picture. We all stood grouped on deck watching it
slowly sink below the horizon. From the first moment that we went on board
all was gay, all luxurious, for were we not guests of a man who, although ab-
surdly economical himself, was always lavish when he entertained? Everyone

was loud in praise of the magnificent appointments of the vessel, and dinner, at which its owner presided, was a merry function.

I was placed next Lord Eldersfield, a pleasant, middle-aged, gray-eyed man, who had recently left the army on succeeding to the title. He was, I found, quite an entertaining companion, full of droll stories and clever witticisms; indeed, he shone at once as the conversationalist of the table.

"Have I been in Algiers before?" he repeated, in answer to a question from me. "Oh, yes. It's a place where one half the people don't know the other half."

I smiled and wondered. Yet his brief description was, I afterwards discovered, very true. The Arabs and the Europeans live apart and are like oil and water, they never mix.

The days passed gayly, and were it not for constant thoughts of that man who had loved me and forgotten I should have enjoyed myself.

Save for one day of mistral the trip across the Mediterranean proved delightful, and for six days we remained in the white old City of the Corsairs, where we went on excursions and had a most pleasant time. We visited the Kasbah, drove to the Jardin d'Essai and to the pretty village of St. Eugène, while several of the party went to visit friends who were staying at the big hotels up at Mustapha. Life in Algiers was, I found, most interesting after the Parisian artificiality and glitter of Nice and Monte Carlo, and with Lord Eldersfield as my cavalier we saw all that was worth seeing. We lounged in those gay French cafés under the date-palms in the Place du Gouvernement, strolled up those narrow, ladder-like streets in the old city, or mingled with those crowds of mysterious-looking veiled Arab women who were bargaining for their purchases in the market. All was fresh, all diverting.

As for Ulrica, she entered thoroughly into the spirit of the thing, as she always did, and with Gerald usually as her escort went hither and thither with her true tourist habit of poking about everywhere, regardless of contagious diseases or the extensive variety of bad smells which invariably exists in an Oriental town. Although each day the party went ashore and enjoyed themselves, old Mr. Keppel never accompanied them. He knew the place, he said, and had some business affairs to attend to in the deck-house which he kept sacred to himself. Therefore he was excused.

"No, Miss Rosselli," he had explained to me in confidence, "I'm no sight-seer. If my guests enjoy seeing a few of the towns on the Mediterranean I am quite contented, but I prefer to remain quiet here rather than to be driving about in brakes and revisiting places that I have already visited long ago."

"Certainly," I said. "You are under no obligation to these people. They accept your kind hospitality, and the least they can do is to allow you to remain in peace when you wish."

"Yes," he sighed. "I leave them in Gerald's charge. He knows how to look after them."

And his face seemed sad and anxious, as though he were utterly forlorn.

Indeed, after a week at sea we saw but little of him. He lunched and dined with us in the saloon each day, but never joined our musical parties after dinner, and seldom, if ever, entered the smoking-room. All knew him to be eccentric, therefore this apparent disregard for our presence was looked upon as one of his peculiar habits. Upon Gerald devolved the duty of acting as entertainer, and assisted by Ulrica, myself, and old Miss Keppel he endeavored to make every one happy and comfortable. Fortunately, the ubiquitous Barnes had by Gerald's urgent desire been left behind at the Villa Fabron.

As day by day we steamed up that blue, tranquil sea in brilliant weather, with our bows ever set in the track of dawn, life was one continual round of merriment from three bells, when we breakfasted, until eight bells sounded for turning in. A yachting cruise is very apt to become monotonous, but on the Vispera one had no time for ennui. After Algiers we put in for a day at Cagliari, then visited Tunis, the Greek islands, Athens, Smyrna, and Constantinople.

We had already been five weeks cruising—and five weeks in the Mediterranean in spring are delightful—when one night an incident occurred which was both mysterious and disconcerting. We were on our way from Constantinople, and in the first dog-watch had sighted one of the rocky headlands of Corsica. That evening dinner had been followed by an impromptu dance which had proved a most successful affair. The men were mostly dancers, except Lord Stoneborough, who was inclined to obesity; and with the piano and a couple of violins played by a pair of rather insipid sisters the dance was quite a jolly one. We even persuaded old Mr. Keppel to dance, and although his was not a very graceful terpischorean feat, nevertheless his participation in our fun put every one in an exceedingly good humor.

Of course, the time had not passed without the usual gossip and tittle-tattle which are inseparable from a yachting cruise. On board a yacht people become quickly inventive, and the most astounding fictions about one's neighbors are whispered behind fans and books. I had heard whispers regarding Ulrica and Gerald Keppel. Rumor had it that the old gentleman had actually given his consent to their marriage, and as soon as they returned to America the engagement would be announced.

Certain of the guests, with an air of extreme confidence, took me aside and questioned me regarding it, but I merely responded that I knew nothing and greatly doubted the accuracy of the rumor. More than once that evening I had been asked whether it were true, and so persistent seemed the rumor that I took Ulrica into my cabin and asked her point-blank.

"My dear," she cried, "have you really taken leave of your senses? How absurd! Of course there's nothing whatever between myself and Gerald. He is amusing, that's all."

"You might do worse than marry him," I laughed. "Remember, you've known him a long time—four years, isn't it?"

"Marry him! Never! Go and tell those prying persons, whoever they are, that when I'm engaged I'll put a paragraph in the papers all in good time."

"But don't you think, Ulrica," I suggested—"don't you think that if such is the case Gerald is rather too much in your society?"

"I can't help him hanging around me, poor boy," she laughed. "I can't be rude to him."

That night I turned and turned in my narrow berth, but could not sleep. The atmosphere seemed stifling in spite of the ventilators, and I dare not open the port-hole, fearing a sudden douche, for a wind had sprung up and we were rolling heavily. The jingle of the glasses on the toilet-stand, the vibration, the throbbing of the machinery, the tramping of the sailors overhead, the roar of the funnels, all rendered sleep utterly impossible.

At last, however, I could stand it no longer, and, rising, I dressed, putting on a big driving-coat, with a thick shawl about my head, and went up on deck. The fresh air might perhaps do me good, I thought. At any rate, it was a remedy worth trying.

The night, so brilliant a couple of hours before, had become dark and stormy, the wind was so boisterous that I walked with difficulty, and the fact that the awnings had been reefed showed that Davis, the skipper, anticipated a squall.

The deck was deserted. Only on the bridge could I see, above the strip of sheltering canvas, two shadowy figures in oilskins keeping watch ahead. Save for those heads I was utterly alone. On my way towards the stern I passed the small deck-house which old Mr. Keppel reserved as his own den. The green-silk blinds were always drawn across the port-holes and the door always remained locked. No one ever entered there, although many had been the speculations regarding the private cabin when we had first sailed.

The millionaire himself had, however, given an explanation one day at luncheon.

"I always reserve, both in my houses and here on board the Vispera, one room as my own. I hope all of you will excuse me this. As you know, I have a good many affairs to attend to, and I hate to have my papers thrown into disorder."

Personally, I suspected him of having a lathe there and of pursuing his hobby of ivory-turning, but the majority of the guests accepted his explanation that this deck-house was his study, and that he did not wish them to pry there.

More than once Ulrica had expressed to me wonder regarding the reason the cabin remained always closed and its curtains always drawn. Every woman dearly loves a mystery, and, like myself, Ulrica, when she discovered anything suspicious, never rested until she had formed some theory or other.

She had one day mentioned the fact to Gerald, who in my presence had given what appeared to me the true explanation.

"It's merely one of the guv'nor's eccentricities. The fact is that on the outward voyage from New York he bought some antique Moorish furniture and ivory carving in Tangier and has it stored in there until we return. I've seen it myself—beautiful things. He says he intends to sell them at a profit to a dealer in London," whereat we laughed.

Knowing how the old gentleman practised economy sometimes, I had accepted this as the truth.

But as, gripping the rail to prevent being thrown down by the rolling of the ship, I passed along the side of the deck-house I was surprised to see a light within. The curtains of green silk were still drawn, but the light could, nevertheless, be seen through them, and it seemed to me strange that any one should be there at that hour of the night. I placed my face close to the screwed-down port-hole, but the curtain had been so well drawn that it was impossible to see within. Then, moving quietly, I examined the other three round, brass-bound windows, but all were as closely curtained as the first.

I fancied I heard voices as I stood there and tried to distinguish the words, but the roar of the funnels and howling of the wind drowned every other sound.

What if my host caught me prying? His private affairs were surely no business of mine, therefore I was about to turn away, when suddenly I experienced an extraordinary desire to peep inside that forbidden chamber. I walked around it again stealthily, for fortunately I was in thin slippers.

While standing there in hesitation I noticed that upon the low roof was a small ventilator which had been raised to admit air. What if I could get a peep down there? It was an adventurous climb for a woman hampered by skirts as I was; but I searched for means to mount, and found them in a low iron staple to which some cords of the rigging were attached and a brass rail which afforded rather insecure foothold. After some effort I succeeded in scrambling to the top, but not before I found myself beneath the eye of the officer on the bridge. Fortunately I was behind him, but if he had occasion to turn towards the stern he must discover me.

Having risked so much, however, I was determined to make further endeavors, and leaning across the small roof I placed my face close to the open ventilator and peered down into the locked cabin.

Next second I drew back with a start, holding my breath. A loud exclamation of dismay escaped me, but the sound was swallowed up in the noises of the boisterous night.

The sight I witnessed below me in that small deck-house held me rigid as one petrified.

CHAPTER XIII
DISCLOSES A MILLIONAIRE'S SECRET

SO HEAVILY WAS THE yacht rolling that I was compelled to hold firmly, lest I should lose my balance and roll down upon the deck.

My foothold was insecure, and the sight which presented itself as I peered within was so unexpected and startling, that in the excitement of the moment I loosened my grip and narrowly escaped being pitched down headlong. From my position I unfortunately could not obtain a view of the entire interior, the ventilator being open only a couple of inches, but what I saw was sufficient to unnerve any woman.

The cabin was brilliantly lit by electricity, but the walls, instead of being panelled in satinwood, as were most of the others, were decorated in a manner more rich and magnificent than in any other part of the vessel. They were of gilt, with white ornamentation in curious Arabesques, while upon the floor was a thick Turkey carpet with a white ground and pattern of turquoise blue. The effect was bright and glaring, and at the first moment it occurred to me that the place was really a ladies' boudoir. There was another aft, it was true, but this one had evidently been intended as a lounge for female guests. As I looked down old Benjamin Keppel himself passed into that part of the cabin within the zone of my vision. His hat was off, displaying his scanty gray hair, and as he turned I caught a glimpse of his face. His countenance, usually so kind and tranquil, was distorted by abject fear; his teeth were set, his cheeks hard and bloodless. Both anger and alarm were depicted upon his rugged countenance. His appearance was mysterious, to say the least, but it was a further object I saw within that place which held me in speechless wonderment.

Beside where he stood, lying in a heap at his feet, was a dark-haired, handsome woman of mature age, who was dressed in a white serge robe—a stranger.

The old millionaire, with sudden movement, flung himself upon his knees and touched her face caressingly. Next instant he drew back his hand.

"Dead!" he gasped, in the thick voice of a man grief-stricken. "Dead! And she did not know—she did not know! It is murder!" he gasped in a terrified whisper—"murder!"

The wind howled about me weirdly, tearing at my clothes as though it would hurl me beyond into the raging sea, while the yacht, steaming on, rose and plunged, shipping huge seas each time her bows met the angry waves.

For some moments the strange old man bent over the woman in silence. I was puzzled to discover her identity. Why had she been kept prisoner in that gilded cabin during the cruise? Why had we remained in total ignorance of her presence? I alone knew our host's secret. We had a dead woman on board.

Keppel touched the woman again, placing his hand upon her face. When he withdrew it I saw that blood was upon it. He looked at it and, shuddering, wiped it off upon his handkerchief.

At the same instant a voice, that of a man, sounded from the opposite side of the cabin, saying:

"Don't you see that that ventilator is open up above? Shut it, or somebody may see us. They can see down here from the bridge."

"Think of her," the old man exclaimed in a low voice, "not of us."

"Of her? Why should I?" inquired the gruff voice of the unseen. "You've killed her, and must take the consequences."

"I?" gasped the old man, staggering unevenly to his feet, and placing both hands to his eyes as though to shut out from view that hideous evidence of his crime. "Yes," he cried in an awe-stricken tone, "she is dead!"

"And a good job too," responded the man unseen in a hard, pitiless tone.

"No," cried Keppel angrily. "At least respect her memory. Remember who she was."

"I shall remember nothing of this night's work," the other responded. "I leave all memories of it as a legacy to you."

"You coward!" cried Keppel, turning upon the speaker, his eyes flashing. "I have endeavored to assist you, and this is your gratitude."

"Assist me?" sneered his companion. "Pretty assistance it's been! I tell you what it is, Benjamin Keppel, you're in a very tight place just now. You killed that—that woman there, and you know what the penalty is for murder."

"I know," wailed the white-faced, desperate man.

"Well, now, if I might be permitted to advise, I'd make a clear sweep of the whole affair," said the man.

"What do you mean?"

"Simply this: we can't keep the body very long in this cabin without it being discovered. And when it is found—well, it will be all up with both of us. Of that there's but little doubt. I suggest this: Let us make at once for one of the

Italian ports, say Leghorn, where you will land to transact some important business, and I'll land also. Then the Vispera will sail for Naples, to which port you will go by rail to rejoin her. On the way there, however, the vessel disappears—eh?"

"Disappears—how? I don't understand."

"Is blown up."

"Blown up!" he cried. "And how about the guests?"

"Guests be hanged!"

"But there are eleven of them, besides the crew."

"Never mind them. There are the boats, and no doubt they'll all take care of themselves. Fools if they don't."

"I should feel that I murdered them all," the old man responded.

"In this affair we must save ourselves," declared the unseen man very firmly. "There has been a—well, we'll call it an ugly occurrence tonight, and it behooves us to get clear out of it. If the Vispera goes down the body will go down with it, and the sea will hide our secret."

"But I cannot imperil the lives of all in that manner. Besides, by what means do you suggest destroying the ship?"

"By perfectly simple means. Just give orders to Davis in the morning to put in at Leghorn with all possible speed, and leave the rest to me. I'll guarantee that the Vispera will never reach Naples." Then he added: "But just shut that infernal ventilator; I don't like it being open."

Old Keppel, staggering, reached the cord, and in obedience to his companion's wish closed the narrow opening with a sudden bang. The woodwork narrowly escaped coming into contact with my face, and for some moments I remained there, clutching at my unstable supports and being rudely buffeted by the gale.

At any moment I might be discovered, therefore after some difficulty I succeeded in lowering myself again to the deck and making my way back to my own cabin.

I had been soaked to the skin by the rain and spray, but, still in my wet things, I sat pondering over the mysterious crime I had discovered.

Who was that unseen man? Whoever he was he held old Benjamin Keppel in his power, and to his diabolical plot would be due the destruction of the Vispera and perhaps the loss of every soul on board.

He had suggested an explosion. He no doubt intended to place on board some infernal contrivance which, after the lapse of a certain number of hours, would explode and blow the bottom out of the yacht. Whoever that man was he was a crafty villain. Providentially, however, I had been led to the discovery of the scheme, and I did not mean that the lives of my fellow-guests or of the crew should be sacrificed in order to conceal a crime.

A vision of that white, dead face recurred to me. It was the face of a woman who had once been very handsome, but to my remembrance I had never seen it before. The mystery of the woman's concealment there was altogether extraordinary. Yet it scarcely seemed possible that she should have remained in hiding so long without a soul on board save Keppel being aware of her presence. She had been fed, of course, and most probably the steward knew of her presence in that gilded deck-house. But she was dead—murdered by the inoffensive old gentleman who was the very last person in the world I should have suspected of having taken human life.

And why had he stroked her dead face so caressingly? Who, indeed, was she?

My wet clothes clung to me cold and clammily, therefore I exchanged them for a warm wrap, and entering my berth tried to rest. Sleep was, however, impossible in that doomed ship amid the wild roaring of the tempest and the thunder of the waves breaking over the deck above. Once it occurred to me to go straight to Ulrica and tell her all I had seen and heard, but on reflection I resolved to keep my own counsel and narrowly watch the course of events.

The mystery of the hidden man's identity grew upon me, until I suddenly resolved to make a further endeavor to discover him. The voice was deep and low, but the roaring of the wind and hissing of escaping steam had prevented me hearing it sufficiently clearly to recognize whether it was that of one of our fellow-guests. I slipped on a mackintosh, and returning to the deck crept towards the cabin wherein reposed the remains of the mysterious woman in white serge. But soon I saw that the light had been switched off. All was in darkness. The guilty pair had gone below to their own berths. Through the whole night the storm continued, but the morning broke brightly and the tempest, as is so frequent in the Mediterranean, was succeeded by a dead calm, so that when we sat down to breakfast we were steaming in comparatively smooth water.

"Have you heard?" said Ulrica across to me after we had been exchanging our sleepless experiences. "Mr. Keppel has altered our course. He has some pressing business to attend to, so we are going into Leghorn."

"Leghorn!" exclaimed Lord Eldersfield at my elbow. "Horrid place! I was there once. Narrow streets, dirty people, primitive sanitation, and a sorry attempt at a promenade."

"Well, we don't stay there long, that's one comfort," said Ulrica. "Mr. Keppel is going to land, and he'll rejoin us at Naples."

I looked down the table and saw that the face of the old millionaire was pale, without its usual composure. He was pretending to be busily occupied with his porridge.

"Are we going on straight to Naples, Keppel?" inquired Eldersfield.

"Certainly," answered our host. "I much regret that I'm compelled to take you all out of our original course, but I must exchange some telegrams with my agent in New York. We shall be in Leghorn tonight, and if you are all agreed you may sail again at once."

"I'd like to see Leghorn," declared Ulrica. "People who go to Italy always leave it out of their itinerary. I've heard that it is quite charming in many ways. All the better-class Italians from Florence and Rome go there for the bathing in summer."

"Which I fear isn't much of a recommendation," observed his Lordship, who was, I believe, Ulrica's pet aversion.

"The bathing itself is declared by all the guide-books to be the best in Europe," she answered.

"And the heat and mosquitoes in summer greater than in any other place on the Continent of Europe. Its imports are rags from Constantinople and codfish from Newfoundland. No wonder its effluvias are not all roses."

"Perhaps so. Of course, if you know the place you are welcome to your own opinion. I don't know it."

"When you do, Miss Yorke, you'll share my opinion; of that I feel certain," he laughed, and then continued his meal.

The question was shortly afterwards decided by popular vote whether the Vispera should remain in Leghorn or not. To the majority of the guests Leghorn was supposed to be merely a dirty seaport, and although I, who knew the place well, tried to impress upon them that it possessed many charms not to be found in other Italian towns, it was decided that the yacht should only remain there a day, and then go straight on to Naples.

This decision was disconcerting. I had to prevent the trip southward, and the problem of how to do so without arousing suspicion was an extremely difficult one to solve. If the vessel sailed from Leghorn, then she was doomed, with every soul on board.

CHAPTER XIV
IN WHICH I MAKE A RESOLVE

THE GREAT BROAD PLAIN which lies between marble-built old Pisa and the sea was flooded by the golden Italian sunset, and the background of the serrated Apennines loomed a dark purple in the distance as we approached the long breakwater which protects Leghorn from the sea.

Leaning over the rail, I gazed upon the white, sun-blanched Tuscan town, and recognized the gay Passeggio with its avenue of dusty tamarisks, its long rows of high white houses with their green persiennes, and Pancaldi's and the other baths, built out upon the rocks into the sea. Years ago, when at the convent, we had gone there each summer, a dozen or so girls at a time, under the kindly care of Suor Angelica, to obtain fresh air and escape for a fortnight or so the intolerable heat of July in the Lily City. How well I remembered that long promenade, the Viale Regina Margherita, but known to those happy, light-hearted, improvident Livornesi by its ancient name, the Passeggio. And what long walks we girls used to have over the rocks beyond Antignano, or scrambling climbs up to the shrine of the miracle-working Virgin at Montenero. Happy, indeed, were those summer days with my girl friends—girls who had now, like myself, grown to be women—who had married, and had experienced all the trials and bitterness of life. A thought of her who was my best friend in those past days recurred to me—pretty, black-haired, unassuming Annetta Ceriani, from Arezzo. She had left the college the same week as myself, and our parting had been a very hard one. In a year, however, she had married, and was now a princess, the wife of Cesare Sigismondo, Prince Regello, who, to give him all his titles, was "Principe Romano, Principe di Pinerolo, Marchese di Casentino, Conte di Lucca, Nobile di Monte Catina." Truly the Italian nobility do not lack titles. But poor Annetta! Her life had been the reverse of happy, and the last letter I had received from her, dated from Venice, contained the story of a woman heart-broken.

Yes, as I stood there on the deck of the Vispera approaching the old sun-whitened Tuscan port many were the recollections of those long-past careless days which crowded upon me, days before I had known how weary was the world, or how fraught with bitterness was woman's love.

Already the light was shining yellow in the high, square old light-house, although the sun had not altogether disappeared. Half-a-dozen fine cruisers of the British Mediterranean Squadron were lying at anchor in line, and we passed several boats full of sun-tanned liberty men on their way to the shore for an evening promenade, for the British man-o'-warsman is always a welcome guest in Leghorn. At last, when within a quarter of a mile of the breakwater, I heard old Mr. Keppel, who stood close to me, speaking to the captain.

"I shall send a couple of packets on board in the morning, and also a box, Davis. Put the latter below in a safe place. Lock it up somewhere."

"Very well, sir," answered the man, in his smart uniform, leaning over the rail of the bridge. "And we sail for Naples after the things are on board?"

"Yes. And wait there for me."

"Very well, sir." And then he turned to give some directions to the helmsman.

The situation was becoming desperate. How was I to act? At least I should now ascertain who had been the old man's companion in the deck-cabin on the previous night, for they would no doubt go ashore together.

Old Mr. Keppel was standing near me, speaking again to the captain, giving him certain orders, when Gerald, spruce as usual in blue serge, came up and, leaning at my side, said:

"Ulrica says you know Leghorn quite well. You must be our guide. We're all going ashore after dinner. What is there to amuse one in the evening?"

"The gay season hasn't commenced yet," I responded. "But there is opera at the Goldoni always. One pays only a dollar for a box to seat six."

"Impossible," he laughed incredulously. "I shouldn't care to sit out music at that price."

"Ah, there I must differ," I replied. "It is as good as any you'll find in Italy. Remember, here is the home of opera. Why, the Livornesi love music so intensely that it is no unusual occurrence for a poor family to make shift with a piece of bread and an onion for dinner in order to pay the fifty centesimi ingresso to the opera. Mascagni is Livornese, and Puccini, who composed 'La Boheme,' was also born close here. No. In 'cara Livorno,' as the Tuscan loves to call it, one can hear the best opera for ten cents."

"Different to our prices in America."

"And our music, unfortunately, is not so good," I said.

"Shall we go to this delightfully inexpensive opera tonight? It would certainly be an experience."

"I fear I shall not," I answered. "I am not feeling very well."

"I'm extremely sorry," he said with quick apprehension. "Is there anything I can get you?"

"No, nothing, thank you," I answered. "A little faintness, that's all."

We had already anchored just inside the breakwater, and a boat had been lowered. Four of the crew were in it, ready to take their owner ashore.

"Good-by—good-by, all!" I heard old Benjamin Keppel saying in his hearty manner, and, turning, met him face to face.

"Good-by, Miss Rosselli!" he shouted to me, laughing as he raised his cap. "I shall be back with you at Naples."

I gripped the rail and acknowledged the salute of the man who was leaving the vessel he had doomed to destruction.

All the guests were on deck, and many were the good wishes sent after him as he sprang into the boat and the men pulled off towards the port. Then a few moments later the bell rang for dinner and all descended to the saloon, eager to get the meal over and go ashore.

On the way down Ulrica took me aside, saying:

"Gerald has told me you are ill, my dear. I've noticed how pale and unlike yourself you've been all day. What's the matter?—tell me."

"I—I can't. At least not now," I managed to stammer, and at once escaped her.

I wanted to be alone to think. Keppel had gone ashore alone. His companion of the previous night, the man to whom the conception of that diabolical plot was due, was still on board. But who was he?

I ate nothing, but was in the first boat that went ashore. I had excused myself from making one of the party at the opera, after giving all necessary directions, and on pretence of going to a chemist's to make a purchase I separated myself from Ulrica, Gerald, and Lord Stoneborough in the Via Grande, the principal thoroughfare.

How next to act I knew not. Keppel had expressed his intention of sending a box on board, and there could be no doubt that it would contain some explosive destined to send the Vispera to the bottom. At all hazards the yacht must not sail. Yet how was it possible that I could prevent it without making a full statement of what I had overheard?

I entered the pharmacy and purchased the first article that came into my mind. Then, returning into the street, I wandered on, plunged in my own distracting thoughts.

The soft, balmy Italian night had fallen, and the white streets and piazzas of Leghorn were filled, as they always are at evening, with the merry, light-hearted crowds of idlers: men with their hats stuck jauntily askew, smoking, laughing, gossiping, and women, dark-haired, black-eyed, the most handsome in all Italy, each with a mantilla of black lace or of some bright-colored silk as a head-covering, promenading and enjoying the refreshing fresco after the toil and burden of the day. None in all the world can surpass in beauty those Tuscan women—dark, tragic, with eyes that flash quickly in love or hatred, with figures perfect, and each with an easy, swinging gait that a duchess might envy. It was Suor Angelica who had once repeated to me the rhyme that one of our old Florentine writers had written of them,—

> "S'è grande, è oziosa;
> S'è piccola, è viziosa;
> S'è bella, è vanitosa;
> S'è brutta, è fastidiosa."

Every type indeed is represented in that long single street at night—the dark-haired Jewess, the classic Greek, the thick-lipped Tunisian, the pale-cheeked Armenian, and the beautiful Tuscan, the purest type of beauty in all the world.

Once again, after those years, I heard as I walked onward the soft sibillations of the Tuscan tongue about me, the gay chatter of that city of sun and sea, where although half the population are in a state of semi-starvation their hearts are still as light as in the days when "cara Livorno" was still prosperous. But, alas! it has sadly declined. Its manufactures, never very extensive, have died out, its merchant-princes are ruined, or have deserted it, and its trade has ebbed until there is no work for those honest brown-faced men who are forced to idle upon the stone benches in the piazza even though their wives and children are crying for bread.

The splendid band of the Bersagliéri was playing in the great Piazza Vittorio, in front of the British Consulate, where the Consular flag was waving because the war-ships were in the port. The music was there in acknowledgment of the fact that the British marine band had played before the Prefecture on the previous evening. The Consulate was illuminated, and at the balcony with a large party was Her Britannic Majesty's Consul himself, the popular Jack Hutchinson, known to every English and American resident throughout Tuscany as the merriest and happiest of good fellows. But I hurried on across the great square, feeling that no time should be lost, yet not knowing what to do.

The mysterious assassination of poor Reggie and the curious events which followed, coupled with this startling discovery I had made on the previous night, had completely unnerved me. As I tried to reflect calmly and logically,

I came to the conclusion that it was eminently necessary to ascertain the identity of the man who held the Steel King beneath his thrall—the man who had suggested the blowing up of the yacht. This man intended, without a doubt, to leave the vessel under cover of night, or if he were actually one of the guests he could, of course, easily excuse himself and leave the others, as I had done.

I entered the Hotel Giappone, where I had once stayed with some friends after leaving the convent, and after succeeding in changing some money, went forth again among the chattering crowd, when suddenly it occurred to me that if our host intended to leave Leghorn he must leave by train. Therefore I entered a tram and alighted at the station. Several trains had, I ascertained, left for Pisa in connection with the main line from Genoa to Rome since Keppel had landed. Perhaps, therefore, he had already left.

The great platform was dimly lit and deserted, for no train would depart, they told me, for another hour. It was the mail, and ran to Pisa to catch the night express to the French frontier at Modane.

Should I remain and watch?

The idea occurred to me that if the unseen individual who had been present in the deck-house intended to come ashore he would certainly meet Keppel somewhere, where the explosive would be prepared and packed in the box ready to be sent on board early in the morning. Most probably the pair would contrive to catch this, the last train from Leghorn. So I resolved to remain.

The time dragged on. The short train was backed into the station, but no passenger appeared. A controller inquired if I intended to go to Pisa, but I replied in the negative. At last one or two passengers approached leisurely, as is usual in Italy, carrying wicker-covered flasks of Chianti to drink en voyage; the inevitable pair of white-gloved carabineers strolled up and down, and the train prepared to start.

Of a sudden, almost before I was aware of it, I was conscious of two figures approaching. One was that of old Mr. Keppel, hot and hurrying, carrying his small hand-bag, and the other the figure of a woman wearing a soft felt hat and long fawn travelling-cloak.

I drew back into the shadow in an instant to allow them to pass without recognizing me, for I had fortunately put on an old black dress which I had never worn on board. The miscreant had, it seemed, cleverly disguised himself as a woman.

Hurrying, they next moment passed me by in search of an empty first-class compartment. The controller approached them and asked for their tickets, when Keppel, feeling in his pockets with fidgety air, answered in English, which, of course, the man did not understand,—

"We're going to the frontier."

The man glanced leisurely at the tickets, then unlocked one of the doors and allowed them to enter.

As the woman mounted into the carriage, however, a ray of light fell straight across her face, and revealed to my wondering eyes a countenance that held me absolutely stupefied.

The discovery I made at that moment increased the mystery tenfold.

CHAPTER XV
IS ASTONISHING

THE COUNTENANCE DISCLOSED BY the lamp in the great ill-lit station was not that of a man in female disguise, as I had suspected, but of a woman. Her identity it was that held me in amazement, for that instant I recognized her as none other than the dark-haired, handsome woman whom I had seen lying dead upon the floor of the deck-house on the previous night.

Why were they leaving the yacht in company? What fresh conspiracy was there in progress?

I had always believed old Benjamin Keppel to be the soul of honor, but the revelations of the past few hours caused me utter bewilderment. I stood there in hesitation, and glancing up at the clock saw that there were still three minutes before the departure of the train.

Next moment I had made a resolve to follow them and ascertain the truth. I entered the booking-office, obtained a ticket to Modane, the French frontier beyond Mont Cenis, and a few moments later was sitting alone in a compartment at the rear of the train. I had no luggage, nothing whatever except the small travelling-reticule suspended from my waist-belt, and I had set out for an unknown destination.

The train moved off, and soon we were tearing through the night across that wide plain which was the sea-bottom in the mediæval days when the sculptured town of Pisa was a prosperous seaport, the envy of both Florentines and Genoese, and past the spot marked by a church where St. Peter is said to have landed. Well I knew that wide Tuscan plain, with its fringe of high, vine-clad mountains, for in my girlhood days I had wandered over it hither and thither in the royal forest and through the smiling vine-lands.

At last, after three-quarters of an hour, we ran into the busy station of Pisa, that point so well known to every tourist who visits Italy. It is the highway to Florence, Rome, and Naples; just as it is to Genoa, Turin, or Milan, therefore as the traveller in Switzerland must at some time find himself at Bâle, so does the traveller in Italy always find himself at Pisa. Yet how few strangers who pass through, or who drive down to look at the leaning tower and the great old cathedral, white as a marble tomb, ever take the trouble to explore the country beyond? They never go up to quiet, gray old Lucca, a town with walls and gates the same today as when Dante wandered there, untouched by the hand of the vandal, unspoilt by modern progress, undisturbed by tourist invaders. Its narrow, old-world streets of decaying palaces, its leafy piazzas, its Lily theatre, its proud, handsome people, all charming to one who, like myself, loves her Italy and the gay-hearted, mirthful Tuscan.

Little time was there for reflection, however, for on alighting at Pisa I was compelled to conceal myself until the arrival of the express on its way from Rome to Paris. While I waited the thought occurred to me that the Vispera was still in peril, and I alone could save her passengers and crew. Yet with the mysterious woman still alive there could, I pondered, be no motive in blowing up the ship. Perhaps the idea had happily been abandoned, and some color was lent to this latter theory by the fact that Keppel had not made any excuse by which to prevent Gerald from travelling farther in the doomed vessel. No father could possibly allow his son to sail in a ship which he intended should never reach port.

Nevertheless, the non-appearance of the individual whose voice I had heard, but whom I had not seen, was disconcerting. Try how I would, I could not get rid of the suspicion aroused by Keppel's flight that foul play was still intended. If it were not, why had not the old millionaire continued his cruise? The unknown woman had been concealed on board for weeks, therefore there was no reason why she should not have remained there for another three days until we reached Naples. No, that some curious mystery was connected with the whole affair I felt confident.

I peered forth from the corner in which I was standing and saw Keppel and his companion enter the buffet. Then, when they had disappeared, I made a sudden resolve, and entering the telegraph office wrote the following message:

To Captain Davis, S. Y. 'Vispera,' in port, Livorno.

"Have altered arrangements. Sail at once for Genoa. Box and packages I spoke of will join you there. Leave on receipt of this.
"Keppel."

I handed it to the telegraphist, saying in Italian, "I want this delivered on board tonight most particularly."

He looked at it and shook his head.

"I fear, Signorina," he answered with grave politeness, "that delivery is quite impossible. It is after hours, and the message will remain in the office and be delivered with letters in the morning."

"But it must reach the Captain tonight," I declared.

The man elevated his shoulders slightly and showed his palms, the Tuscan gesture of regret.

"At Livorno they are not, I am sorry to say, very obliging."

"Then you believe it to be absolutely useless to send the message, expecting it to be delivered before morning?"

"The Signorina understands me exactly."

"But what am I to do?" I cried in desperation. "This message must reach the Captain before midnight."

The man reflected for a moment. Then he answered,—

"There is but one way I can suggest."

"What is that?" I cried anxiously, for I heard a train approaching, and I knew it must be the Paris express.

"To send a special messenger to Livorno. A train starts in half-an-hour, and the message can then be delivered by half-past eleven."

"Could you find me one?" I asked. "I'm willing to bear all expenses."

"My son will go, if the Signorina so wishes," he responded.

"Thank you so much," I replied, a great weight lifted from my mind. "I leave the matter entirely in your hands. If you will kindly see that this message is delivered you will be performing not only myself but a number of other persons a very great service."

"The Signorina's instruction shall be obeyed," he answered, and having placed some money to cover expenses upon the counter, I again thanked him and left, feeling that, although I had been guilty of forgery, I had, nevertheless, saved the yacht from destruction.

The train with its glaring head-lights swept into the station from its long journey across Maremma marshes, but I saw with considerable dismay that there was but one sleeping-car, the only through car for the frontier. I was therefore compelled to travel in this, even at the risk of meeting Keppel in the corridor. One cannot well travel in one of those stuffy cars of the Compagnie International des Wagon-Lits without being seen by all one's fellow-travellers, and here my first difficulty presented itself.

I watched the old gentleman and his companion enter the car, and from the platform saw them shown their respective berths by the conductor. Keppel was given a berth in a two-bed compartment with another man, while the tall, dark woman was shown to one of the compartments set aside for ladies at the other end of the car.

With satisfaction I watched the old millionaire take his companion's hand and wish her good-night, and then, when his door had closed, I myself mounted into the car and demanded a place.

"The Signorina is fortunate. We have just one berth vacant," answered the man in Italian. "This way, please," and taking me along the corridor he rapped at the door of the compartment to which he had just shown the mysterious woman.

There was the sound of quick shuffling within, the door was opened, and I found myself face to face with her.

I left it to the conductor to explain my presence, and entering, closed and bolted the door behind me.

"I regret that I have been compelled to disturb you, but this is the only berth vacant," I said in English in a tone of apology, for I noticed that her black eyes flashed inquiringly at me, and therefore deemed it best to be on friendly terms with her.

"Don't mention it," she answered quite affably. "I'm pleased that you're English. I feared some horrid foreign woman would be put in to be my travelling-companion. Are you going far?"

"To the frontier," I responded vaguely. The extent of my journey depended upon the length of hers.

Then after a further exchange of courtesies we prepared for the night, and entered our narrow berths, she choosing the upper one and I the lower.

As far as I could judge she was nearly fifty, still extremely handsome, her beauty being of the Southern type, and her black hair and coiffure, with huge tortoise-shell comb, giving her a Spanish appearance. She wore several beautiful rings, and I noticed that on her neck, concealed by day by her bodice, was some tiny charm suspended by a thin golden chain. Her voice and bearing were those of an educated woman, and she was buxom without being beefy.

The roar of the train and the grinding of the wheels as we whirled through those seventy-odd tunnels that separate Pisa from Genoa rendered sleep utterly impossible, so by mutual consent we continued our conversation.

She seemed like the "Ancient Mariner"—needing some one to whom she could tell her story. She needed an audience who could realize the fine points of her play. From the first she seemed bursting with items about herself, little dreaming that I was acting as spy upon her. I secretly congratulated myself upon my astuteness, and proceeded to draw her out. Her slight accent puzzled me, but it was due, I discovered, to the fact that her mother had been Portuguese. She seemed to label everything with her own intellectual acquirements. To me, a perfect stranger, she chatted during that night journey about her fine figure and her power over men,—about her ambitions and her friends; but her guardian interfered with her friends. He, her guardian, was an old man and jealous, had her money invested in America, and would not allow her to look at a man. If she did look at men she received no money. She was not forty, she told me, and he, her guardian, who was also in the train, was over seventy.

When she was not telling me the story of her loves, and her father, mother, and step-father, she filled in the time by telling me about some man whom she called Frank, who had a pretty-faced wife addicted to the illicit consumption of brandy.

"Trouble?" she wandered on. "Oh, I've had such lots and lots of it that I'm beginning to feel very old already. Troubles I always think are divided into two classes—one controlled by a big-horned, cloven-hoofed devil, and the other by the snippy little devil that flashes in and out of our hearts. The big devil is usually placed upon us by others."

I laughed, admitting that there was much truth in her words.

"And the other—the little imp?" I asked.

"The other? This insane perversity of human nature gets hold of us whether we will or not. It makes us for the time ignore all that is best in ourselves and in others—it is part of us. Though we know well it is all within ourselves, it will cause our tears to flow and our sorrows to pile up. It is all a fictitious substance with possibly a mint of happiness lying below. We are conscious of it all, but the insanity makes us ignore it for so long that the little imp completes its work, and the opportunity is lost. But why are we moralizing?" she added. "Let's try and get to sleep, shall we?"

To this I willingly acquiesced, for, truth to tell, I did not give credence to a single word of the rather romantic story she had related regarding herself, her friends, and her jealous guardian. I had met women of her stamp many times before. The only way to make them feel is to tell them the truth, devoid of all flattery.

She struck me as a woman with a past—her whole appearance was of such. Now a woman with a checkered past and an untrammelled present is always more or less interesting to women as well as men. She is a mystery. The mystery is that men cannot quite believe that a smart woman with knowledge cut loose from all fetters is proof against flattery. She "queens" it while they study her. Interest in a woman is only one step from love for her—a fact of which we of the fairer sex are very well aware.

Ulrica had once expressed an opinion that pasts were not so bad if it were not for some of the memories that cling to them, not, of course, that the past of either of us had been anything out of the ordinary. Memories that cling to others or the hint of a "past" certainly make you of interest to others, especially to men, and a menace to the imagination of other women; but the memories that hover about yourself are sometimes like truths—brutal.

Memories! As I lay there upon my hard, narrow bed, being whirled through those suffocating tunnels in the cliffs beside the Mediterranean, I could not somehow get away from memory. The story this mysterious woman had related had awakened all the sad recollections of my own life. It seemed as though an avalanche of cruel truths confronted my mental vision. At every instant those truths struck a blow that left a scar deep and unsightly as any made by the knife. There was tragedy in every one. The first that came to me was of a day long ago. Ah me! I was young then, a child in years, a novice in experience, on that day when I admitted to Ernest my deep and fervent affection. How brief it all had been! I had, alas! now awakened to the hard realities of life and to the anguish the heart is capable of holding. The sweetest part of love, the absolute trust, had died long ago. My heart had lost its lightness never to return, for his love for me was dead. His fond tenderness of those by-gone days was, alas! only a memory.

Yet he must have loved me! With me it had been the love of my woman-hood—the love that is born with youth, that overlooks, forgives, and loves again; that gives friendship, truth, and loyalty. What, I wondered, were his thoughts when we had encountered each other at Monte Carlo? He showed neither interest nor regret. No, he had cast me aside, leaving me to endure that crushing sorrow and brain-torture which had been the cause of my long illness. He remembered nothing. To him our love was a mere incident. Of a verity, memory is the scar of truth's cruel wound.

I lay there wondering to myself if ever again I should feel any uplifting joy or any heartrending sorrow. Ah! if women could only outgrow the child part of their natures, hearts would not bleed so much. One of the greatest surprises in life is to discover how much sorrow the heart can bear, how acutely it can ache, how it can be strained to the utmost tension, crowded with agony, and yet not break. This is moralizing and smacks of sentiment, but it is nature—after you get acquainted with it.

The train roared on, the woman above me slept soundly, and with the tears starting in my eyes I tried hard to burn the bridges into the past and seek for-getfulness in sleep. The process of burning, alas! can never be accomplished, thanks to one's too retentive memory, but slumber came to me at last, and I must have dozed some time, for when I awoke we were in Genoa, and daylight was already showing through the chinks of the crimson blinds.

But the woman who had told the curious story slept on. Probably the concoction of so much romantic fiction had wearied her brain. The story she had related could not, of course, be true. If she were really old Keppel's ward, then what motive had he in concealing her in that gilded deck-house which was believed to be stored with curios? Who too was that unseen man whom he had apparently taken into his confidence—the man who had promised assistance by blowing up the yacht with all hands?

I shuddered at thought of that wicked, dastardly plot.

Yet Keppel had been declared by this unknown person to be the murderer of the woman now lying in the berth above me. Why?

The train was at a stand-still, and I rose to peep out. As I turned to re-enter my berth again my eyes fell upon the sleeping form of my companion. Her face was turned towards me, and her bodice, unhooked, disclosed a delicate white throat and neck.

I bent quickly to examine more closely what I saw there. Upon the throat were two dark marks, one on either side,—the marks of a human finger and a thumb,—the exact counterpart of those puzzling marks found upon the throat of poor Reggie.

CHAPTER XVI
IS MORE ASTONISHING

SO STILL, SO PALE, so bloodless were my mysterious companion's lips, that at the first moment I feared she might be dead. Her appearance was that of a corpse, but after careful watching I saw that she was breathing, lightly but regularly, and thus I became satisfied.

The curious marks, as though a man's hands had endeavored to strangle her, were of a pale yellowish brown, like disappearing bruises, the one narrow and small where the finger had pressed, the other wide and long, the mark of the thumb.

Again I returned to my berth, and as the express again thundered on its way northward towards Turin, I tried to form some theory to account for my discovery of those curious marks upon her.

The hours of early morning crept slowly by. The sun rose over the beautiful vine-lands of Asti as we whirled forward towards the great Alpine barrier which happily divides Italy from France; its rays penetrated into our narrow chamber, but the sleeping woman stirred not. She seemed as one in a trance.

Close beside me lay her dress-skirt. My eyes had been fixed upon it a hundred times during the night, and it now occurred to me that by searching its pocket I might discover something that would give a clue to her real identity. Therefore, after ascertaining that she was still unconscious of things about her, I slowly turned over the skirt, and placing my hand in the pocket drew out the contents.

The first object I opened was a silver-mounted purse of crocodile leather, hoping to discover her visiting-card therein. But in this I was disappointed. The purse contained only a few francs in French money, a couple of receipts from shops in Paris, and a tiny scrap of card an inch square with several numerals scribbled upon it.

The numbers were unintelligible, but when I chanced to turn the piece of thin pasteboard over its reverse gave me an instant clue. It was a piece of one of those red-and-black ruled cards used by gamblers at Monte Carlo to register the numbers at roulette. This woman, whoever she was, had evidently been to Monte Carlo, and the numbers scribbled there were those which she believed would bring her fortune. Every woman gambler has her strong-rooted fancies, just as she has her amusing superstitions, and her belief in unlucky days and unlucky croupiers.

Two facts were plain. First, that she bore marks upon her which were the exact counterpart of those found on poor Reggie; secondly, that she herself had been to Monte Carlo.

Her handkerchief was of fine lawn, but bore no mark, while the crumpled piece of paper—without which no woman's pocket is complete—proved on examination to contain only an address of some person in Brussels.

I therefore carefully replaced them all, having failed to ascertain her name, and then dozed again.

She was already up and dressed when I awoke.

"Ah!" she laughed, "I see you've been sleeping well. I've had a famous night; I always sleep well when I travel. But I have a secret. A doctor friend of mine gave me some little tabloids of some narcotic,—I don't know its name,—and if I take one I sleep quite well for six or seven hours at a stretch."

"I awoke once, and you were quite sound asleep."

"Oh, yes," she laughed. "But I wonder where we are?"

I looked forth and recognized the name of some small station through which we dashed.

"We're nearing Turin," I responded. Then suddenly recollecting that in an hour or so I should be compelled to face old Keppel in the corridor, I resolved on a plan upon which I immediately proceeded to act. "I don't feel at all well this morning," I added. "I think I shall go to sleep again."

"I've some smelling-salts here," she said, looking at me with an expression of sympathy. And she took out a small silver-mounted bottle from her little reticule.

I took it and sniffed it gladly with a word of thanks. If I did not wish to meet Keppel, I should be obliged to remain in that stuffy little den for another twenty hours or so—that is, if they intended to go on to Paris. The prospect was certainly not inviting, for a single night in a Continental sleeping-car over a badly laid line gets on one's nerves terribly. Compelled, however, to feign illness, I turned in again at Turin, and while my companion went forth and rejoined the man who had been my host the conductor brought me the usual glass of hot coffee and a roll.

"I am not well," I explained to the man when he handed it to me. "Are you going through to Paris?"

"Sì signorina."

"Then will you see that I'm not disturbed, either at the frontier or anywhere else?"

"Certainly—if the Signorina has the keys of her baggage."

"I have no baggage," I responded. "Only see that I get something to eat, and buy me a novel—Italian—French—anything will do, and also some newspapers."

"Sisignorina." And the door was closed.

Five minutes later, just as the train was gliding out of Turin, the man returned with a couple of novels and half-a-dozen of those four-paged badly printed Italian newspapers, and with them I managed to while away the long, tedious hours as we sped through Susa and the beautiful Alpine valleys.

From time to time my companion looked in to see how I was, offering to do anything for me that she could; then she returned to old Keppel, who was sitting on one of the little flap-seats in the corridor smoking.

"The woman in with me is rather young and quite charming," I heard her say to him. "She's been taken queer this morning. I expect the heat has upset her, poor thing! The berths here are very hot and close."

"Horribly! I was nearly asphyxiated," he answered.

Then, about half-an-hour later, I recognized his voice again. He was evidently standing with his companion close to the door of my compartment.

"We shall be in Paris about half-past eight tomorrow morning, it seems," he said.

"And the Vispera will be awaiting you at Naples?" she laughed.

"Davis is quite used to my erratic movements," he answered. "A reputation for eccentricity is very useful sometimes."

"But shall you rejoin her?"

He hesitated.

"I think it is most unlikely," he responded. "I've had enough of cruising. You too must be very tired of it."

"Tired!" she cried. "Imprisoned in that cabin all day long, with the windows closed and curtained, I felt that if it lasted much longer I must go mad. Besides, it was only by a miracle that I was not discovered a dozen times."

"But, very fortunately, you were not," he said.

"And all to no purpose," she observed in a tone of weariness and discontent.

"Ah! that's quite another matter—quite another matter."

"I do wish that you would satisfy my curiosity and tell me what occurred on the night before we landed," she said. "You know what I mean."

She evidently referred to the attempt upon her life.

"Well," he responded in hesitation, "I myself am not quite clear as to what took place. I entered the cabin, you know, and found you lying unconscious."

"Yes, I know. I was thrown violently down by a sudden lurching of the ship, and must have struck my head against something," she replied. "But afterwards I remember experiencing a most curious sensation in my throat, just as though some one with strong, sinewy fingers were trying to strangle me. I have the marks there now."

"Absurd!" he laughed. "It was only your imagination. The close confinement in that place together with the rolling of the ship had caused you a little light-headedness, without a doubt."

"But it was more than imagination, of that I feel certain. There was blood upon my lips, you remember."

"Because in falling you had cut your lower lip. I can see the place now."

"I believe that some one tried to take my life."

"Rubbish! Why, whom could you suspect? I was the only soul on board who knew of your presence there. Surely you don't suspect me of attempted murder?"

"Of course not," she answered decisively.

"Then don't give way to any wild imaginings of that sort. Keep a cool head in this affair."

The remainder of the conversation was lost to me, although I strained my ears to catch every sound. His words made it plain that she was in ignorance of the knowledge possessed by the unseen man whose voice I had overheard, and further that both were acting in accord in order to obtain some object the nature of which was to me a complete mystery.

She came a short time afterwards and inquired kindly how I felt. They were going to change into the dining-car, and she hoped I would not starve altogether. As I talked to her I recollected the strange marks I had seen upon her throat—those distinct impressions of finger and thumb. I looked again for them, but they were concealed by the lace of her high-necked bodice. There seemed a strange, half-tragic beauty about her face. She was certainly fifty, if not more, yet in the broad daylight I could detect no thread of silver in her hair. She was extremely well-preserved.

The conductor brought me a cutlet and a bottle of Beaujolais after we had passed through the Mont Cenis, and for some hours afterwards I lay, reading and thinking. We were on our way to Paris, but with what motive I had no idea.

I wondered what they would think on board the Vispera when they found me missing, and laughed aloud when I reflected that the natural conclusion would be that I had eloped with old Mr. Keppel. I rather regretted that I had told Ulrica nothing, but of course a telegram to her would explain everything on the morrow. The yacht would be lying safely in Genoa harbor awaiting her owner, who never intended to return.

And where was the unseen man? That was a puzzling problem which I could not solve. I could not even form the slightest theory as to whom he might really be.

The day passed slowly and evening fell. We were nearing Culoz. The woman with the mysterious marks upon her returned with her escort from the dining-car and sat chatting with him in the corridor. Their voices reached me, but I could distinguish little of their conversation. Suddenly, however, I thought I could hear a third voice in conversation, the voice of a man.

It sounded familiar; I listened again. Yes, it seemed as though I had heard that voice somewhere before. Indeed, I knew its tone perfectly well.

For some minutes I lay listening, trying to catch the words. But the train was roaring through a deep cutting, and I could only hear disjointed words or parts of sentences.

In determination to see who it was I carefully opened the door of the compartment so that I could peer through the chink.

I bent forward until my eyes rested upon the speaker, who, lounging near, was engaged in serious confidential conversation with Keppel and my travelling-companion, as though they were old friends.

In an instant I drew back and held my breath. Was this the man who had suggested the blowing up of the Vispera? Surely not. Perhaps, however, he had actually travelled with us from Pisa in another carriage, or perhaps he had joined the train at some intermediate station. But by whatever means he had come there, the fact of his identity remained the same.

It was Ernest Cameron, the man I loved.

CHAPTER XVII
CONFIDES THE STORY OF A TABLE

THE DISCOVERY OF ERNEST'S presence in the car was an entirely fresh development of the mystery. I had been ignorant of his acquaintance with Keppel, but that they were really close friends was evident by the rapid, rather apprehensive manner in which they were conversing.

I tried, and tried again, to overhear some of the words spoken, but in vain. Therefore I was compelled to remain in wonderment until the conclusion of that long, terribly tiring journey half way across Europe.

Arrived at the Gare de Lyon in Paris, I entered a fiacre and followed them across the city to the Hotel Terminus, that big caravansary outside the Gare St. Lazare, where they engaged four rooms on the first floor—a sitting-room and three bedrooms. Having taken every precaution to prevent being detected by either of them, I ascertained that the number of the sitting-room was 206, therefore I engaged 205, the room adjoining, and ordered a light déjeûner to be taken there. I was faint, nervous, and tired after being cramped up for thirty hours, and was resting on the couch, when suddenly voices sounding in the next room caused me to spring up on the alert in an instant.

Keppel and Ernest were speaking together.

"It's a risk, of course," the millionaire was saying in a low voice—"a great risk."

"But we've run greater in this affair," the other responded. "You know how near to arrest I have been."

I held my breath. Arrest! What could he mean?

"It was fortunate that you escaped as you did."

"Thanks to you. Had you not concealed me on the Vispera and taken me on that cruise I should now be in the hands of the police."

"But they seem to possess no clue," Keppel observed.

"Fortunately for us, they do not," answered the man to whom I had given my heart. And he laughed lightly, as though perfectly confident in his own safety. "It was that transfer of the notes at the Carnival ball that puzzled them."

They were speaking of poor Reggie's murder!

I held my ear close to the dividing door, striving to catch every word. I was learning their secret! The two men whom I had least suspected were actually implicated in that dastardly crime. But what, I wondered, could have been their motive in taking the poor boy's life? Certainly robbery was not the incentive, for to the old Pittsburg inventor sixty thousand francs was but a paltry sum.

Again I listened, but as I did so the woman entered, and then, taking leave of her, the two men went forth and down the stairs.

In an instant I resolved to follow them, and ere they had gained the entrance-hall I had put on my hat and descended. They took a cab, and first drove up the hill behind St. Lazare to the Boulevard des Batignolles, descending before a large house where, from an old concierge in slippers, Ernest received two letters. Both men stood in the door-way and read the communications through. From their faces I could see that the letters contained serious news, and for some minutes they stood in indecision.

At length, however, they re-entered the cab and drove back past the Opera, through the Rue Rivoli, and across the Pont des Arts, turning into a labyrinth of narrow, dirty streets beyond the Seine, and stopping before a small, un-inviting-looking hairdresser's shop.

They were inside for some ten minutes or so, while I stood watching a short distance off, my head turned away, so that they should not recognize me if they came forth suddenly.

When they emerged they were laughing good-humoredly, accompanied to the door by a rather well-dressed man, evidently a hairdresser, for a comb protruded from his pocket and his hair was brushed up in that style peculiar to the Parisian coiffeur.

"Good-day, messieurs," he said in French, bowing them into the fiacre, "I understand quite clearly. There is nothing to fear, I assure you, absolutely nothing."

In that man's dark eyes, as he stood watching the cab turning, was a strange, intense look which struck me as familiar. Yes, I had seen those eyes before, without a doubt. His face was triangular, with broad forehead and pointed chin—a rather curious personality. Again I looked at his peculiarly brilliant eyes, and a strange truth flashed suddenly upon me. Yes, I remembered that curious expression quite distinctly; it had riveted itself indelibly upon my memory.

He was the man who had worn the owl's dress in Carnival—the man who had returned to me the notes stolen from poor Reggie! He was an accomplice of these two men, of whom I had never entertained suspicion.

The truth came to me as a staggering blow. Ernest was an assassin! Had he not admitted how near he had been to arrest and congratulated himself upon his escape? Had not old Keppel aided him by concealing him on board the Vispera? Once, alas! I had, in my foolish, rosy days of youth, believed in the man who had made love to me, who had flattered and caressed me, and who had declared that I should be his always. Ah! how well I remembered it! How bitterly all the past came back to me! And yet, until that very hour of my discovery that he was an assassin, I had never ceased to love him—never for a single instant. We women are indeed strange creatures.

I re-entered the cab, but in the Boulevard St. Michel my driver unfortunately lost sight of them. They must, I think, have turned suddenly into one of the many side-streets and thus reached the Quai.

For a few minutes I sat back in hesitation. Should I return at once to the hotel? or should I go boldly to that man whom I had so fortunately discovered and charge him with having had in his possession the stolen notes? If I adopted the latter course I saw that I should only raise an alarm, and the pair I was watching would undoubtedly get clean away. No, the old proverb that "murder will out" had once more asserted its truth. I had made a most amazing discovery, and now my love for Ernest as a man having been transformed to hatred of him as an assassin, I meant to weave a web slowly about them, and when complete I would give information to the police and thus avenge the poor boy's death.

Therefore I drove to the nearest telegraph office and wired to Genoa, urging both Ulrica and Gerald to come to Paris without delay, for I sorely needed the counsel of the woman who was my best friend and the man upon whose father rested the terribly strong suspicion. Then I returned to the Hotel Terminus, and, hearing no one in the sitting-room adjoining, lay down to rest, sleeping soundly, for with nerves unstrung, I was utterly worn out by fatigue and constant watchfulness.

When I awoke it was past eight o'clock and quite dark. There was still no movement in the sitting-room adjoining, therefore I dressed and went across to dine at the Duval, at the corner of the Rue du Havre, preferring that cheap restaurant to the table d'hôte of the hotel, where I might possibly meet the three persons upon whom I was keeping observation.

An hour later, just as I was crossing the road to re-enter the hotel, I saw a man standing alone on the steps in hesitation. He wore a dark beard, and had on a long drab overcoat such as men generally affect on race-courses, but notwithstanding the disguise I recognized that it was Ernest. The beard made him look much older, and by the addition of a few lines to his face he had entirely altered his appearance. For some moments he puffed pensively at his cigar, then, glancing at his watch, descended the steps and strolled slowly away, past the Café Terminus—which was once the object of a desperate attack by Anarchists—and continued along the Boulevard des Capucines, where he stopped before that popular rendezvous of Parisians, the Grand Café, and selecting one of the tables, the last one towards the Madelaine, placed against the wall of the Café, he ordered a coffee and liqueur. The night was bright, and the grand boulevards with their blazing globes of electricity were full of life and movement.

From where I was sitting, at a small brasserie on the opposite side of the boulevard, I watched him narrowly. He glanced up and down, as though in constant expectation of meeting some one, and looked at his watch impatiently. He tossed off his liqueur at a single gulp, but his coffee remained untasted, for it was evident that he was in a state of the greatest agitation. He had feared arrest for the murder of Reginald Thorne, and had taken refuge secretly on the Vispera. Were not his own words sufficient to convince me of his guilt?

As I looked I saw him, while in the act of pretending to sip his coffee, bend down close to the marble table, and after making certain that he was not observed, he scrutinized it carefully. Twice he bent to look at it closely. Surely, I thought, there must be something of interest there. Then he glanced at his watch again, paid, and strolled off down the boulevard.

Whether to follow or whether to investigate that table I was for the moment undecided. But I resolved upon the latter course; therefore, crossing the road, I made straight for the seat he had occupied, and having ordered a sirop proceeded to examine the table. Very quickly I discovered what had interested him. Scrawled in pencil upon the marble were some letters quite unintelligible, but evidently a cipher message. It ran—

"J. Tabac. 22."

Another inscription had been written there, but it had been lately erased by some previous customer, who had apparently dipped his fingers in the drippings of beer or coffee and smeared it across. The writing was not very easy to discern in the half light, for the table was so placed as to be in deep shadow. Was it possible that the person who had erased the first message had written the second? Could it be that this person was the man whom I had been watching?

I had seen him bend over the table mysteriously, first glancing round to make sure that no one was watching. Why had he thus betrayed fear if that message was not one of importance? Goron, the great chief of the Paris sureté, had told me, when I had met him at dinner once in New York, how the criminals of Paris were fond of making the tops of the café tables the means of secret communications, and how many a crime had been discovered by the police with the aid of the keys they possessed to certain secret codes.

I looked again at the initial, the word "tobacco," and the number twenty-two scrawled on the marble before me, and was puzzled to know what meaning they could convey. Had Ernest really written them? The letters were printed, in order, no doubt, to prevent any recognition of the handwriting. I remembered that he had sat with his hand upon the table as though toying idly with the matches, and further I noticed that the liquid with which the erasure had been made was not yet entirely dry. I touched it with my gloved finger and placed it to my nose. There was an odor of coffee.

Now if Ernest had really inscribed that cipher message he had substituted his for the original one written there. With what purpose? To whom was this unintelligible word addressed? Having regard to the fact that the tables of cafés are usually washed down by the waiters every morning, it seemed certain that the person to whom he intended to convey the message would come there that night. Indeed, he had constantly looked at his watch, as though in expectation of the arrival of some one.

I therefore paid the waiter and left, returning some few minutes later to my previous place in front of the brasserie opposite, determined to wait and watch. The waiter brought me some illustrated papers, and while pretending to be absorbed in them I kept my eye upon the table I had just vacated. A shabby, wizen-faced little man in a silk hat with flat brim passed and re-passed where I was sitting, and I thought eyed me rather suspiciously. But perhaps it was only my fancy, for when one is engaged in the work of bringing home to a criminal his crime, one is apt to look with undue suspicion on all and sundry. I think I must have been there nearly half-an-hour when a ragged, unkempt man, who had slunk past where I was seated and picked up several cigar-ends with a stick bearing a sharpened wire point, crossed over to the Grand Café and recommenced his search beneath the tables there. He had secured several pieces of smokers' refuse when, in a moment, he darted to the table in the shadow, and as he stooped, feigning to pick up a piece of unconsumed cigar, I saw that he glanced eagerly to see what message was written there.

Just at that moment the wizen-faced man who had evinced such an extraordinary interest in myself was standing idly upon the curb close by. He was undoubtedly watching him.

The quick eyes of the old collector of cigar-ends apparently understood the message in an instant, for with bent back he continued his active search, yet betrayed no further interest in that table in the shadow. If he had really gone there in order to ascertain the nature of the message, he concealed his real purpose admirably. Probably he was used to being watched by police agents. I saw him hobble along from café to café, his shrewd, deep-set eyes peering from beneath his gray, shaggy brows in search of the tiny pieces discarded by smokers.

With him also disappeared the shabby little man whose interest I had unwittingly aroused, and I remained there still, irresolute and wondering.

I had paid, and was just about to rise and go, when of a sudden a well-appointed victoria pulled up in front of the Grand Café, and from it stepped a small, well-dressed woman wearing a smart hat and an elaborate cape of the latest mode. Without hesitation she walked to the table in question and seated herself. In the darkness I could not distinguish her face, but I saw that even before the waiter could attend to her she had examined the table and read the message thereon written.

Was it, I wondered, intended for her?

The waiter brought what she ordered, a "bock," that favorite beverage with both Parisians and Parisiennes, and as I watched her narrowly I saw something which convinced me that the cipher was intended for her eye. She dipped her finger in the beer and drew it across the writing.

Was she young or old, I wondered? She was settling her cape and chiffons preparatory to rising and re-entering her carriage, therefore I rose and crossed the road. As I stepped upon the asphalte on the opposite side, she crossed to where her smart turn-out stood, brushing past me as she did so.

The light as it fell across her face revealed a countenance with which I was, alas! too familiar.

She was the woman who had usurped my place in Ernest's heart—the woman whom I had seen in his company at Monte Carlo—the woman who had laughed at me in triumph across the roulette table, because she knew that she held him beneath the spell of her extraordinary beauty.

CHAPTER XVIII
GIVES THE KEY OF THE CIPHER

I WALKED ALONG THE boulevard towards the Opera as one in a dream. To that woman with the tow-colored hair, the blue eyes, and pink cheeks—the woman who had replaced me in his affections—he had written that strange message in cipher—a message of warning, it might be. I hated her. I really believe that if ever the spirit of murder has entered my heart it was at that moment. I could have sprung upon her and killed her as she stepped into her carriage.

She had said no word to her coachman. He apparently knew where to drive. That cipher was, perhaps, an appointment which he had gone forward to keep, while she was now following. The thought convulsed me with anger. This man, Ernest Cameron, the man who had once held me in his arms and declared that he loved me, was, upon his own admission, an assassin.

Along the Rue Auber I wandered back to the hotel plunged in my own distracting thoughts. I had somehow ceased to think of the old millionaire and the chattering woman whom he had concealed on board the Vispera. All my thoughts were of the man who had until then held me as his helpless slave.

It may have been jealousy, or it may possibly have been the revulsion of feeling that had seized me on becoming aware of the terrible truth of his guilt, that caused me to vow to leave no stone unturned to secure his arrest and condemnation. She, that small, slim woman with the fair hair, had stolen him from me, but I determined that she should not be allowed to enjoy his society longer. I had discovered the truth, and the blow that I intended to deal would be fatal to the happiness of both of them.

I laughed within myself. I was not impatient. No. I would wait and watch until I had secured ample proof. Then I had but to apply to the police, and the arrest would be made. He, Ernest Cameron, had murdered and robbed the poor boy who had admired me and with whom I had so foolishly flirted. Was it the attention I had allowed him to pay me that was primarily the cause of his assassination? Did the moral responsibility rest upon myself?

That night, even though tired out, I slept but little. Times without number I tried in vain to solve the secret of that cipher message—or warning, was it?—written upon the table before the Grand Café. But neither the initial nor the word "tobacco" conveyed to me any meaning whatsoever. One fact seemed strange, namely, the reason that the ragged collector of cigar-ends should have searched for it, and, further, that the word written there should have been "tobacco." Again, who was the shabby, wizen-faced individual who had also watched that table with such eagerness and expectancy? As I reflected I became impressed by the idea that the table itself was one of those known to be a notice-board of criminals, and therefore at night observation was kept upon it.

The great Goron, that past-master in the detection of crime, had, I remembered, told me that in all the quarters of Paris, from the chic Avenue des Champs Elysées to the lower parts of Montmartre, there were certain tables at certain cafés used by thieves, burglars, and other such gentry for the exchange of messages, the dissemination of news, and the issue of warnings. Indeed, the correspondence on the café tables was found to be more rapid and far more secret, and to attract less attention than the insertion of paragraphs in the advertisement columns of the newspapers. Each gang of malefactors had, he told me, its own particular table in its own particular café, where any number could sit and read in silence the cipher notice or warning placed there without the risk of direct communication with his companions.

Had this man whom I had fondly loved actually allied himself with some criminal band so that he knew their means of communication and was in possession of their cipher? It certainly seemed as though he had. But that was one of the points I intended to clear up before denouncing him to the police.

Next morning I rose early, eager for activity, but there seemed no movement in the room adjoining mine. All three took their coffee in their bedrooms, and it was not until nearly eleven o'clock that I heard Keppel in conversation with the mysterious woman who had been my travelling-companion.

"Ernest is running a great risk," he was saying. "It's quite unnecessary, to my mind. The police are everywhere on the alert, for word has of course come from Nice. If he does, unfortunately, fall into their hands, he'll only have himself to blame."

"But surely you don't anticipate such a thing?" she asked in genuine alarm.

"Well, he goes about quite openly, well knowing that his description has been circulated through every town and village in France."

"And if he were arrested, where should we be?" inquired the woman in dismay.

"In a very awkward predicament, I fear," he responded. "That's the very reason why I'm trying to persuade Cameron to act with greater discretion.

He's well known, you see, and may be recognized at any moment in the street. If he were a stranger here, in Paris, it might be different."

"It's absurd, certainly, for him to run his head into a noose. I must speak to him at once."

"He's out. He went out before six this morning, the chambermaid tells me."

"That's odd! Where's he gone?"

"I don't exactly know. Somewhere in the country, I should think."

"What if he is already arrested?"

"No, don't let's anticipate such a contretemps. Matters are, however, beginning to look serious enough, in all conscience," he answered.

"Do you think we shall succeed?" she inquired eagerly.

"We have been successful before," he responded confidently, "why not now? We have only to exercise just a little more care and cunning than that exercised by the police. Then, once above suspicion, all the rest is perfectly plain sailing."

"Which means that we must make a perfect coup."

"Exactly. The whole scene must be carried out firmly and without a hitch, otherwise we shall find ourselves in very evil case."

"Knowing this should make us desperate," she observed.

"I'm desperate already," he replied in a quiet voice. "It will not go well with any one who tries to thwart us now. It's a matter of life or death."

What new plot had been hatched I could not guess. What was this fresh conspiracy that was intended? His carefully guarded words aroused within me an intense curiosity. I had already overheard many things, and still resolved to possess myself in patience and continue my ever-watchful vigil. There was, according to the old man's own words, a desperate plot in progress, which it was intended to be carried out at all hazards—even to the taking of another human life.

I wrote down on a piece of paper the cipher which I had found scrawled upon the table and tried by several means to reduce it to some intelligible message, but without success. It was evidently in one of those secret codes used by criminals, therefore how could I hope to discover a key to what so often had puzzled the cleverest detectives of the sureté?

The day passed without further incident. I remained in my room awaiting the return of the man whose strange action had so puzzled me on the previous night and who was now running such risk of arrest. If he returned I hoped to overhear his conversation with his companions, but, unfortunately, he did not come back. All was quiet in the adjoining chamber, for Keppel and the woman with the strange marks had evidently gone out in company.

About seven o'clock I myself dressed and went forth, wandering idly down until I stood on the pavement at the corner of the Boulevard des Italiens, before the Opera. There are always many idlers there, mostly sharks on the look-out for the unsuspecting foreigner. The English and American tourist offices are just opposite, and from the corner these polyglot swindlers easily fix upon likely victims and track them down. Suddenly it occurred to me to stroll along and glance at the table before the Grand Café. This I did, but found only the remains of some cipher which had been hastily obliterated, possibly earlier in the day, for the surface of the marble was quite dry, and only one or two faint pencil-marks remained.

As I sat there I chanced to glance across the road, and to my surprise saw the same shabby, wizen-faced man lounging along the curb. He was evidently keeping observation upon that table.

In pretence of not seeing him, I drank down my coffee, paid, and rising walked away. But he at once followed me, therefore I returned to the hotel. It is not pleasant to a woman to be followed by a strange man, especially if one is bent upon making secret inquiries or watching another person, so when I had again returned to my room I presently bethought myself of the second exit from the hotel—the one which leads straight into the booking-office of the Gare St. Lazare. By this door I managed to escape the little man's vigilance, and entering a cab drove down to the Pont des Arts. I had nothing particular to do, therefore it occurred to me that if I could find that little coiffeur's where I had seen the man with whom I had danced on the night of the Carnival ball, I might watch and perhaps learn something. That this man was on friendly terms with both Keppel and Cameron had been proved by that scrap of confidential conversation I had already overheard.

The difficulty I experienced in recognizing the narrow, crooked street was considerable, but after nearly an hour's search through the smaller thoroughfares to the left of the Boulevard St. Michel my patience was rewarded, and I slowly passed the little shop on the opposite side. The place was in darkness, apparently closed. Scarcely had I passed, however, when some one emerged from the place, and turning I saw it was the man who had worn the owl's dress. He was attired smartly, and seemed to possess quite an air of distinction. Indeed, none meeting him in the street would believe him to be a barber.

Almost involuntarily I followed him. He lit a cigarette and then walked forward at a rapid pace down the boulevard across the Pont Neuf, and turning through many streets, which were as a bewildering maze to me, suddenly tossed his cigarette away, entered a large house, and made some inquiry of the concierge.

"Madame Fournereau?" I heard the old man answer gruffly. "Yes. Second floor, on the left."

And the man who had so mysteriously returned to me the stolen notes went forward and up the stairs.

Madame Fournereau? I had never, as far as I recollected, heard that name before.

I strolled along a little farther, hesitating whether to remain there until the man emerged again, when lifting my eyes I saw the nameplate at the street-corner. It was the Rue du Bac. In an instant the similarity of the word in the cipher, "Tabac," occurred to me. Could it be that the woman for whom the message was intended lived there? Could it be that this woman for whose love Ernest had forsaken me was named Fournereau? I entertained a lively suspicion that I had at last discovered her name and her abode.

I think that at that moment my usual discretion left me utterly. So many and so strange were the mysteries which had surrounded me during that past month or so that I believe my actions were characterized by a boldness of which no woman in her right senses would have been capable. Now that I reflect upon it all, I do not think that I was in my right senses that night, or I should never have dared to act alone and unaided as I did. But the determination to avenge the poor lad's death and at the same time to avenge my own wrongs was strong upon me. A jealous woman is capable of breaking any of the ten commandments. Amor dà per mercede, geliosa è rotta fede.

Had I reminded to reason with myself I should never have entered that house, but fired by a determination to seek the truth and meet that woman face to face, I entered boldly, and without a word to the concierge passed up to the second floor.

The house was, I discovered, like many in Paris, of a character superior to what its exterior denoted. The stairs leading to the flats were thickly carpeted and were illuminated by electricity, whereas from the street I had believed it to be a house of quite a fourth-rate class. When I rang at the door on the left a neat bonne in a muslin cap answered my summons.

"Madame Fournereau?" I inquired.

"Oui, madame," answered the woman, and admitting me to the small but well-furnished entrance-hall, waved her hand forward, saying: "Madame is expecting you, I believe. Will you please enter?"

My quick eyes noticed in the hall a number of men's hats and women's capes, and from the room beyond came quite a babble of voices. I walked forward in wonderment, but next second knew the truth. The place was a private gambling-house. Madame's guests, a strange and motley crowd, came there to play games of hazard.

In the room I entered was a roulette table, smaller than those at Monte Carlo, but around it were some twenty men and women, all intent upon the game. Notes and gold were lying everywhere upon the numbers and the simple chances, and the fact that no silver was there was sufficient testimony that high stakes were usual. The air was close and oppressive, for the windows were closed and heavily curtained, and above the sound of excited voices rose that well-known cry of the unhealthy-looking, pimply-faced croupier in crumpled shirt-front and greasy black,—

"Messieurs, faites vos jeux!"

Advancing to the table, I stood there unnoticed in the crowd. Those who saw me enter undoubtedly believed me to be a gambler like themselves, for it appeared as though Madame's guests were drawn from various classes of society. The atmosphere was stifling, but excited as I was I managed to remain cool and affect an interest in the game by tossing a louis upon the red.

I won. Strange how carelessness at roulette invariably brings good fortune.

I glanced about me, eager to discover Madame herself, but saw neither her nor the barber whom I had followed there. At the end of the room there were, however, a pair of long, sage-green curtains, and as one of the players rose from the table and passed between them I saw that another gaming-room lay beyond, and that in there they were playing baccarat, the bank being held by a superior-looking old gentleman with the crimson ribbon of the Legion d'Honneur in the lapel of his dining-jacket.

Boldly I went forward into that room, and in an instant saw that I was not mistaken, for there, chatting to a circle of men and women at the opposite end of the salon, was the small, fair-haired woman whom I had seen in Ernest's company at Monte Carlo. The man who had given me the stolen notes was standing in the crowd about her, and to them she was recounting the story of a pleasure trip from which she had apparently only just returned.

A couple of new-comers, well-dressed men, entered, and walking straight to her shook her hand, expressing delight that she had returned to Paris to resume her entertainments.

"I too am glad to return to all my friends, messieurs," she laughed. "I really found Monte Carlo very dull after all."

"You were not fortunate? That is to be regretted."

"Ah!" she said, exhibiting her palms. "With such a maximum how can one hope to gain? It is impossible."

I stood watching the play. As far as I could see it was perfectly fair, but some of the players, keen-faced men, were evidently practised card-sharpers, swindlers, or men who lived on their wits. The amount of money constantly changing hands surprised me. As I stood there one young man, scarcely more than a lad, lost five thousand francs with the most perfect sang-froid. The women present were none of them young, but were mostly elderly and ugly, of that stamp so eternally prominent in the Principality of Monaco. The woman, when she turns gambler, always loses her personal beauty. It may be the vitiated atmosphere in which she exists, it may be the constant tension of the nerves, or it may, perchance, be the unceasing, all-consuming avarice, which I know not. All I am certain of is that no woman can play and at the same time remain fresh, youthful, and interesting.

Until that moment I had remained there unnoticed in the excited crowd, for I had turned my back upon Madame Fournereau, lest she should recognize in me the woman whom Ernest had undoubtedly pointed out to her either in the Rooms, in Ciro's, or elsewhere.

But as I advanced to pass back to the adjoining room, where I considered there would be less risk of recognition, the long green curtains suddenly opened and Ernest Cameron stood before me.

CHAPTER XIX
PIECES TOGETHER THE PUZZLE...

I STEPPED BACK QUICKLY, while he, with eyes fixed upon that fair-haired woman, who seemed the centre of a miniature court, failed to notice me. Upon his face was a dark, anxious look, an expression such as I had never seen there before. Perhaps he was jealous of the attentions shown by the dozen or so of men who were chatting and laughing with her.

Her appearance was scarcely that of the keeper of an illicit gambling-house. One would have expected to find some fine, dashing, handsome woman in a striking gown and profuse display of jewelry. On the contrary, she was quietly dressed in a pretty, graceful gown of dove-gray cashmere, the bodice cut low and trimmed with silver passementerie, a frock which certainly well became her rather tame style of beauty. Her only ornament was a small half-moon of diamonds in her hair.

Ernest, on entering, appeared to recognize the situation at a glance, and with his back turned to her stood watching the baccarat just as I had feigned to watch. Through the great mirror before him, however, he could note all her actions. She was laughing immoderately at some remark made by one of her companions, and I noticed how Ernest's face went pale with suppressed anger. How haggard, how thin, how blanched, nervous, and ill he looked! Usually so smart in attire, his dress-clothes seemed to hang upon him, his cravat was carelessly tied, and in place of the diamond solitaire I had bought at Tiffany's for him in the early days of our acquaintance,—which he had still worn when we met at Monte Carlo,—there was only a common, plain pearl stud, costing perhaps ten centimes. Alas! he had sadly changed. His was, indeed, the figure of a man haunted by the ever-present shadow of his crime.

Curious, I thought, that he did not approach her, but the reason for this became plain ere long. I had returned to the adjoining room and was again watching the roulette, when she brushed past me on her way out into the corridor, from which led off several other rooms, and suddenly I heard his well-known voice utter her name in a hoarse whisper,—

"Julie!"

She stopped, and recognizing him for the first time, gasped,—

"Ernest! You here?"

"Yes," he responded. "I told you that we should meet, and I have found you, you see. I must speak to you alone."

"Impossible," she responded. "Tomorrow."

"No—to-night—now. What I have to say admits of no delay," and he strode resolutely at her side, while she, her face betraying displeasure at the encounter, unwillingly went forth into the corridor.

"Well?" I heard her exclaim in impatience. "And what is it you have to say to me? I thought when we parted it was not to meet again."

"You hoped so, you mean," he answered hardly. "Come into one of these rooms where we may be alone. Someone may overhear if we remain here."

"And is it so strictly confidential, then?"

"Yes," he answered, "it is." Then, with great reluctance and impatience, she opened a door behind them and they passed into what appeared to be her own petit-salon.

Again the fire of jealousy consumed me, and without thought of the consequences of my act, I went straightway to the door and entering faced them.

As I entered Ernest turned quickly, then stood rigid and amazed.

"Carmela!" he gasped. "How came you here—to this place?"

"How I came here matters not," I answered in a hard tone. "It is sufficient for you to know that I have entered here to demand an explanation from you and this woman, your accomplice."

"What do you mean?" cried his companion in her broken English. "What do you mean by accomplice?"

"I refer to the murder of Reginald Thorne," I said, as quietly as I was able.

"The murder of Monsieur Thorne," repeated the woman. "And what have I to do, pray, with the death of that gentleman, whoever he may be?"

Ernest glanced at me strangely, then addressing her in a firm voice said,—

"The woman who murdered him was yourself—Julie Fournereau."

I stood dumfounded. Was it possible that he intended to endeavor to fix the guilt upon her, even though I knew the truth by the admission I had overheard?

"What!" she shrieked in fierce anger, speaking in French. "You have sought me here to charge me with the murder?—to bring against me a false accusation? It is a lie! You know that I am innocent."

"That point, madame, must be decided by a judge," he answered with marvellous coolness.

"What do you mean? I don't understand!" she exclaimed with a slight quiver in her voice which betrayed a sudden fear.

"I mean that during the months which have elapsed since the murder of my friend Thorne at Nice I have been engaged in tracing the assassin—or, to put it plainly, in tracing you."

I stood there utterly astounded. If his words were true, why had he been concealed on board the Vispera in order to avoid arrest?

She laughed, instantly assuming an attitude of defiance.

"Bah!" she said. "You bring me here into this room to make this absurd and unfounded charge. You dare not say it before my friends. They would beat you like the hound you are."

His cheeks were pale, but there was a fierce, determined expression upon his countenance. The woman whom I had believed he loved was, it seemed, his bitterest enemy.

"I have no wish whatever to bring upon you any greater exposure or disgrace than that which must inevitably come," he said coolly. "For months I have been awaiting this opportunity, and by the cipher fortunately discovered your return. I was then enabled to give the police some highly interesting information."

"The police!" she gasped, her face instantly blanched to the lips. "You have told them?"

"Yes," he responded, gazing steadily upon her, "I have told them."

"Then let me pass," she said hoarsely, making towards the door. But in a moment he had barred her passage, and raising a small whistle quickly to his lips blew it shrilly.

"So this is your revenge!" cried the miserable woman, turning upon him with a fierce, murderous light in her eyes. Yet ere the words had left her mouth there were sounds of scuffling and shouting, a smashing of glass, and loud imprecations. The whistle had raised the alarm, and the police had entered the place, barring the egress of the players.

Outside in the corridor there were several fierce scrimmages, but next instant the door opened and there entered three detectives, of whom one was the wizen-faced little man who had betrayed such an interest in myself when at the Grand Café, accompanied by old Mr. Keppel and the woman who had been my travelling-companion in the wagon-lit. Certainly the arrangements made by the police to raid the place had been elaborately prepared, for at the signal given by Ernest the coup was complete, and the players, nearly all of whom were persons known as criminals, fell back entrapped and dismayed.

The old millionaire and his companion were as astounded at finding me present as Ernest had been. But there was no time at that exciting moment for explanations. The plan had apparently been arranged for the arrest of the pale, white-faced woman now trembling before us.

"I tell you it's a lie!" she cried hoarsely. "I did not kill him!"

But Ernest, turning to the shabby little man, said,—

"I demand the arrest of that woman, Julie Fournereau, for the murder of Reginald Thorne at the Grand Hotel in Nice."

"You know her," inquired the detective, "and you have evidence to justify the arrest?"

"I have evidence that she committed the murder—that the sixty thousand francs stolen from the dead man's pockets were in her possession on the following morning, and, further, that on the night on which the murder was committed she was staying under another name at the same hotel wherein Mr. Thorne was found dead."

"And the witnesses?"

"They are already in Paris, awaiting to be called to give evidence."

A dead silence fell, and we looked at one another.

The wretched woman who had so suddenly been denounced by the man with whom she had been so friendly at Monte Carlo was standing in the centre of the room, swaying to and fro, supporting herself by clutching the edge of the small table. Her white lips trembled, but no word escaped them. She seemed rendered speechless by the suddenness of the overwhelming charge.

The detective's hard voice broke the silence.

"Julie Fournereau," he said, advancing a few steps towards her, "in the name of the law I arrest you for the murder of Reginald Thorne at Nice."

"I am innocent!" she cried hoarsely, her haggard eyes glaring at us with a hunted look in them. "I tell you I am innocent!"

"Listen," said Ernest in a firm tone, although there was a slight catch in his voice which told how excited he was. "The reasons which have led me to this step are briefly these. Last December I crossed from New York to Havre, and went south to spend the winter at Monte Carlo. I stayed at the Métropole, and amid the cosmopolitan crowd staying there met the woman before you. One day there arrived at the same hotel from Paris my friend, Reginald Thorne, whom I knew well in New York, but who had lived here in Paris for the past year. We were about together during the day, and in the Rooms that evening he encountered me walking beside this woman Fournereau. That same night he came to my room, and in confidence related me a story which at the moment I regarded as somewhat exaggerated, namely, how he had been induced to frequent a certain gaming-house in Paris where he had lost almost everything he possessed, and how he had ultimately discovered that an elaborate system of sharping had been practised upon him by this woman and a male accomplice. That woman, he told me, had left Paris suddenly just at the moment when he discovered the truth, and he had encountered her in the Rooms with me—her name was Julie Fournereau."

I glanced at the wretched woman before us. Her wild eyes were fixed upon the carpet, her fingers were twitching with intense agitation, her breath came and went in short, quick gasps. Ernest in his exposure was, indeed, merciless.

"Had she seen him in the Rooms?" I inquired.

"Yes," he answered. "We had come face to face. He told me that, having been robbed of nearly all he possessed, he was determined to give information against her. She was, he told me, an associate of bad characters in Paris, and urged me to cut her acquaintance. His story was strange and rather romantic, for he gave me to understand that this woman had made a pretence of loving him, and had induced him to play here, in her house, and lose large sums to the men who were her accomplices. Personally, I was not very charmed with her," Ernest went on, glancing at me. "She was evidently, as Thorne had declared, acquainted with many of the worst characters who frequent Monte Carlo, and I began to think seriously that my own reputation would be besmirched by being seen constantly in her company. Still, I tried to dissuade my friend from endeavoring to bring justice upon such a person, arguing that, having lost the money in a private gaming establishment, he had no remedy at law. But he was young and headstrong—possibly suffering from a fit of jealousy. After several days, however, fearing that he might create a scene with this notorious woman, I induced him to go over to Nice and stay at the Grand. While there, curiously enough, he met the lady who is here present, Miss Rosselli, and at once fell deeply in love with her."

"No," I protested in quick indignation. "There was no love whatever between us. That I strongly deny."

"Carmela," he said, addressing me with a calm, serious look, "in this affair I must speak plainly and openly. I myself have a confession to make."

"Of what?"

"Listen, and I'll explain everything." Then, turning to the others, he went on: "Reginald fell violently in love with Miss Rosselli, not knowing that she had once been engaged to become my wife. When, the day after meeting her at the hotel, he told me of his infatuation and I explained the truth, he seemed considerably upset. 'She loves you still,' he said. 'I feel certain that she does, for she has given me no encouragement.' I affected to take no notice of his words, but to me the matter was a very painful one. I had broken off the engagement, it was true, but my heart was now filled with bitter remorse. I had seen Carmela again, all the old love had come back to me, and I now despised myself for my mean and unwarrantable action. We had met several times, but as strangers, and knowing her proud spirit I feared to approach her, feeling certain that she would never forgive."

"Forgive!" I cried. "I would have gladly forgiven."

"Carmela," he said, turning again to me with a grave, serious expression, "I regret being compelled to lay bare my secret thus before you, but I must tell them everything."

"Yes," I said. "Now that this woman is to bear the punishment of her crime, let us know all." Then I added bitterly, "Speak, regardless of my feelings, or even of my presence."

"A few days prior to his tragic end poor Reggie had, as I have explained, moved over to the Grand at Nice, but, strangely enough, the same idea had occurred to this woman Fournereau. She preferred to live in Nice during Carnival, she told me, for she liked all the fun and gayety. Whether it was for that reason I know not, but at all events it seems clear, from inquiries recently completed in Nice, that one afternoon he met this woman at Rumpelmeyer's, the fashionable lounge for afternoon tea, and in a sudden fit of anger declared that he would denounce her as an adventuress and swindler. Now it appears that her clients, the gamblers who frequent this place, number among them some of the most notorious and desperate members of the criminal fraternity, and the natural conclusion is that, fearing his exposure, she killed him."

"I deny it!" cried the wretched woman. "It is a false accusation which you cannot prove!"

"The extreme care and marvellous ingenuity by which the young man's death was encompassed is shown by every detail of the case. Not a single point, apparently, was overlooked. Even the means by which he was assassinated has remained until now a mystery. But, passing to the night of the tragedy, it will be remembered that he had won sixty thousand francs at roulette, and having left Miss Rosselli and her friends he re-entered the Rooms and changed his winnings into large notes. Half-an-hour before, this woman, whom I had met earlier in the evening, and who had dined with me at Ciro's, had wished me good-by, and having previously watched his success at the tables, followed him into the Casino when he re-entered to change the notes. The interval of about an hour between his leaving Monte Carlo and his arrival at the Grand Hotel at Nice is still unaccounted for. Nevertheless, we know that this woman whom he had threatened travelled by the same train from Monte Carlo to Nice, that she entered the hotel a few minutes later and went to her room, and that next morning she had in her possession sixty notes, each for one thousand francs. It seems, however, that she quickly feared that suspicion might rest upon her, for the police had commenced active inquiries, and therefore resolved to get rid of the stolen notes. This she

did with the aid of an accomplice, a man named Laumont, well known at
Monte Carlo each season. This man, one of the habitués of this place, went
to the Carnival ball at the Nice Casino and there gave Miss Rosselli the stolen
money, intending that its possession should throw suspicion upon her. Some
other members of this interesting gang of sharpers who make this place their
head-quarters and who go south in winter in search of pigeons to pluck,
knowing Laumont's intention, posed as detectives, however, and to them
Miss Rosselli innocently handed over the notes she had received."

He paused for a moment, then continued:

"Now, however, comes one of the most ingenious features of the affair. This
woman, finding next day that her plot to throw suspicion upon Miss Rosselli
had failed, turned her attention to myself. She was aware that a slight quarrel
had arisen between Reggie and myself regarding his injudicious and futile
action in seeking to denounce her, and with others had overheard some high
words between us when we had met at the Café de Paris on the day previous
to his death. She gave information to the police, and then left the Riviera
suddenly. Next day I found myself under observation, and in order to escape
arrest induced Mr. Keppel, who has taken a great interest in the affair from
the first, and who is one of the trustees under the will of Mr. Thorne, Senior,
to conceal me on board his yacht until such time as our inquiries in Paris could
be completed. It was ascertained that this woman Fournereau, who had gone
to Russia, intended to return to her apartments here upon a date she had
arranged with her accomplice, Laumont, therefore I have remained in hiding
from the police until today. This is her first reception, notice of which was
circulated among her friends by means of cipher upon certain tables in the
cafés on the grand boulevards."

"But this lady?" I inquired, indicating the handsome woman who had been
my travelling-companion in the wagon-lit.

"I am the mother of Reginald Thorne," she herself responded.

"You Reggie's mother!" I cried, scarce able to believe her words.

"Yes," she answered. "Hearing of my poor son's death, I crossed from New
York to Havre and arrived in Nice only to find that the Vispera had sailed. A
letter was awaiting me with full explanation, asking me to travel to Marseilles
and cross by the mail-steamer to Tunis and there join the yacht. This I did, but
in order that my presence should not be known to those on board I was placed
secretly in the deck-cabin and never went forth. The blow that had fallen
upon me on hearing of poor Reggie's death, combined with the constant
imprisonment in that cabin, I believe upset the balance of my mind, for one
night, the night before we put into Leghorn, I became unconscious. I was

subject to strange hallucinations, and that night experienced a sensation as though some one was attempting to take my life by strangulation."

"I must explain," said old Mr. Keppel, addressing her. "It is only right that you should now know the truth. On the night in question you were unusually restless, and becoming seized by a fit of hysteria commenced to shout and shriek all sorts of wild words regarding your poor son's murder. Now I had concealed you there, and fearing lest some of the guests should hear you and that a scandal might be created, I tried to silence you. You fought me tooth and nail, for I verily believe that the close confinement had driven you insane. In the struggle I had my hands over your mouth and afterwards pressed your throat in order to prevent your hysterical shrieks, when suddenly I saw blood upon your lips, and the awful truth dawned upon me that I had killed you by strangulation. Tewson, the chief steward,—who in addition to Cameron was the only person on board who knew of your presence,—entering at that moment, made the diabolical suggestion that in order to get rid of the evidence of my crime I should allow him to blow up the ship. This I refused, and fortunately an hour later we succeeded in restoring you to consciousness. Then we landed at Leghorn on the following evening, not, however, before I discovered that the real motive of Tewson's suggestion was that he had stolen three thousand pounds in cash, notes, and securities from a despatch-box in Lord Stoneborough's cabin, and wished to destroy the ship so that his crime might remain concealed. The man, I have discovered, has a very bad record, and he has now disappeared."

Then briefly I explained what I had seen and overheard on that wild, boisterous night in the Mediterranean; how I had followed the millionaire and the woman who was bent upon avenging the murder of her son; how I had sent the yacht to Genoa, and how carefully I had watched the movements of all three during those two never-to-be-forgotten days in Paris. All seemed amazed at my story, Ernest most of all.

"During that night in the wagon-lit," I said, addressing Mrs. Thorne, "I noticed two curious marks upon your neck. Upon your poor son's neck were similar marks."

"Yes," she replied, "they were birth-marks—known as the marks of thumb and finger. Poor Reggie bore them exactly as I do." And she also explained how, having recognized me as a fellow-guest on board the Vispera, she had purposely endeavored to mislead me by her conversation, as she feared that my suspicion of Ernest might upset their plans.

"And the woman who murdered poor Reggie, and who so ingeniously attempted first to fasten the guilt upon Miss Rosselli, and afterwards upon myself, is there!" cried Ernest, pointing at the trembling, white-faced figure before us. "She killed him because she feared the revelations he could make to the police regarding this place in which we are standing."

Outside sounded loud scuffling and altercation, for, as it afterwards proved, the strong body of police who had raided the place, finding many persons "wanted," were making wholesale arrests.

The woman Fournereau raised her head at Ernest's denunciation and laughed a strange, harsh laugh of defiance.

"Bien!" she cried shrilly with affected carelessness. "Arrest me, if you will! But I tell you that you are mistaken. You have been clever,—very clever, all of you,—but the assassin was not myself."

The police officer addressed her, saying:

"Then if not yourself, you are aware of the identity of the murderer. So I shall arrest you as being an accomplice. It is the same."

"No, I was not even an accomplice," she protested quickly. "I may be owner of this place; I may be a—a person known to you, but I swear I have never been a murderess."

The officer smiled dubiously.

"The decision upon that point must be left to the judges," he answered. "There is evidence against you. For the present that is sufficient."

"Monsieur Cameron has told you that I was threatened with exposure by the young American gentleman," she said. "That is perfectly the truth. Indeed, all that has been said is the truth—save one thing. I did not commit the murder, nor had I any knowledge of it until afterwards."

"But the stolen notes were actually in your possession on the following morning," the detective observed in a tone of doubt.

"They were given to me for safe-keeping."

"By whom?"

"I refuse to say."

The detective shrugged his shoulders, and a smile passed across the faces of his two companions.

"You prefer arrest, then?" he said.

"I prefer to keep my own counsel," she answered. "These persons," she continued, indicating us, "have believed themselves extremely ingenious, apparently taking upon themselves the duties of the police, and have arrived at a quite wrong conclusion. You may therefore arrest me if you wish. I have nothing whatever to fear."

And she glanced around at us in open defiance. Indeed, so indifferent was she that I felt convinced that Ernest's theory of the committal of the crime had fallen to the ground.

The detective seemed, however, well aware of the character of the woman, and proceeded to deal with her accordingly.

"You are charged with the murder," he said. "It is for you to prove your innocence."

"Who, pray, is the witness against me?" she cried indignantly.

"Your accomplice," cried Ernest quickly. "The man Laumont—the man to whom you gave the stolen notes to transfer to Miss Rosselli."

"Laumont!" she cried. "He—he has told you that I committed the crime—he has denounced me as the murderess?"

"He has," answered Ernest. "On that fatal night when Thorne entered the Rooms to change the notes I met him, and although we had had a few high words in the Café de Paris on the previous day, he approached me, asking my pardon, which I readily gave. He then inquired whether it was really true that Miss Rosselli had been engaged to me. I replied in the affirmative, and he then said that he did not intend to meet her again, but should leave for Paris in the morning. I tried to dissuade him, but his only reply was 'She loves you still, my dear fellow. She can never forget you. Of that I'm certain.' Then he left, and travelled to Nice without further word to her. Arrived at the hotel, he went straight to her sitting-room and sat down to write her a letter of farewell. He commenced one, but destroyed it. This was afterwards found in the room. Then, just as he was about to commence a second letter, you—you, Julie Fournereau—entered, killed him, and stole the notes which you knew he carried in his pockets!"

"How did I kill him?" she demanded, her eyes flashing with anger.

"You yourself know that best."

"Ah! And Jean Laumont told of this elaborate piece of fiction, did he? It is amusing—very amusing!"

At word from the chief detective one of the officers went forth. We heard Laumont's name shouted loudly outside the room, and a few moments later he was ushered in by two officers.

He drew back in quick surprise on seeing us, but in an instant the woman flew at him in fury.

"You have told them!" she shrieked. "You have led them to believe that I murdered the American at Nice—you have declared that it was I who gave you the notes—I who killed him! You miserable cur!"

His countenance fell. Indignation had in an instant given place to fear.

"And did you not give me the notes?" he inquired. "Why, there are at least two men in yonder room who were present when you handed them to me."

"I do not deny that," she responded. "I deny that I killed him."

"Then who did?"

"Who did?" she shrieked. "Who did? Why, you, yourself!"

"You lie!" he cried fiercely, his face ashen pale.

"I would have told them nothing," she went on quickly. "I would have allowed them to arrest me and afterwards discover their mistake, were it not that you had endeavored to give me into their hands in order to save yourself. No, my dear friend, Julie Fournereau is loyal only to those who are loyal to her, as many have before found out to their cost. I would have saved you had you not led the police here to raid my house, to arrest my guests, and to hurry me away to prison for a crime that I did not commit. But listen! You deny the murder of the young American. Well, shall I relate all that occurred?"

"Tell them what untruths you like," he growled. "You cannot harm me."

"Yes, madame," cried old Mr. Keppel. "Tell us all that you know. We are determined now to get to the bottom of this affair."

"This man," she explained, "was the man who fleeced the unfortunate gentleman here in my house. I am not wishing to shield myself for a single moment—I desire only to tell the truth. M'sieur Thorne, when they last met here, accused him of cheating at baccarat, high words ensued, and the young man drew a revolver and fired, striking Laumont in the shoulder. Whereupon the last-named swore to be avenged. I knew well that a vow of vengeance taken by such a desperate man as Laumont was something more than mere idle words, and when he went to the Riviera, as he did each year in search of inexperienced youths whom he could fleece, I shortly afterwards followed. He stayed first at the Hôtel de Paris at Monte Carlo, but meeting young Thorne accidentally one afternoon he discovered that the latter was living at the Grand at Nice, and that same night he transferred his quarters there. Now Thorne had an intimate friend in Nice—Mr. Gerald Keppel—and it seemed as though Laumont desired to make the latter's acquaintance with the ulterior motive of practising his sharper's tricks upon him. Be that how it may, I, in order to watch the progress of events, moved to the same hotel at Nice. I knew that Laumont was bent on vengeance, and felt certain that some terrible dénouement was imminent."

She paused and glanced around at us. Then, lowering her eyes, she went on:

"I am an adventuress, it is true, but I have still a woman's heart. I was determined, if possible, to prevent Laumont from wreaking vengeance upon the poor boy. It was for that reason I followed him to Nice and took up my abode there. On the afternoon of the tragedy I was in the Rooms at Monte Carlo and there saw him playing and winning, while just as he was leaving with Miss Rosselli, another lady, and young Mr. Keppel, his pockets bulging with his gains, I saw Laumont watching him. I knew by the evil look he cast in his direction that the spirit of murder was in his heart. That evening I dined at Ciro's with M'sieur Cameron, and afterwards left him in order to watch the movements of Laumont and the young American. The latter, after a short conversation with M'sieur Cameron in the atrium of the Casino, descended the lift to the station and took train to Nice. I travelled by the same train, but in the crowd at Nice station on alighting lost sight of him. He must have taken a cab immediately to the hotel, and, furthermore, Laumont must also have followed him without knowing of my presence. I met some friends at the station, but on arrival at the hotel twenty minutes later I went straight up to my room. On the way I had to pass the door of Miss Rosselli's sitting-room, and just as I was approaching, my feet falling softly on the thick carpet of the corridor, the door opened noiselessly and a man, after looking forth stealthily, emerged and stole along to the room he occupied. That man was Jean Laumont."

"You saw him!" cried Ernest. "You actually saw him coming from the room?"

"Yes. Instantly I suspected something wrong, and wondered for what purpose he had been in the lady's sitting-room. Therefore without hesitation I pushed open the door and looked inside. Judge my surprise when I found the unfortunate young man writhing in agony on the ground. I knelt by him, but recognizing me as the woman at whose house he had been cheated he shrank from me. 'That man!' he gasped with difficulty,—'that man has killed me!' and a few moments later his limbs straightened themselves out in a final paroxysm of agony and he passed away."

Mrs. Thorne burst into a flood of tears.

The voluble Frenchwoman was silent for a moment, her eyes fixed upon the face of the man against whom she had uttered that terrible denunciation.

"I stood there terrified, unable to move," she went on. "Laumont had, as I feared, killed him."

"Killed him? How can you prove it?" demanded the cunning card-sharper, who, in order to throw the police off the scent, pursued the harmless calling of hairdresser in that back street off the Boulevard St. Michel. "How can you prove it?"

CHAPTER XX
REVEALS THE TRUTH

The woman Fournereau crossed the room quickly to a small rosewood bureau and took therefrom a little card-board box about a couple of inches square, such as are used for cheap jewelry.

"I have something here," she said, addressing the man before her. "It was lying on the floor. You alone knew its secret—a secret which I too have lately discovered."

And opening the box carefully she displayed, lying in a bed of cotton-wool, what at first appeared to be a woman's steel thimble. Taking it from its hiding-place and putting it upon the fore-finger of her right hand, we saw that, instead of being what it at first appeared, it rose to a sharply tempered steel point about half an inch long protruding from the finger-tip.

I glanced at the man accused. His face had blanched to the lips at sight of it.

"This," she explained, "I discovered on the floor close to where the dead man was lying. It is a diabolic invention of Laumont which he showed me a year ago, although he did not then explain its use. An examination which has been made by a friend, a chemist, has shown plainly the truth. You will notice that the point is fine as a needle, but is hollow, like that of a hypodermic syringe. Within, at the point touched by the tip of the finger, is a small chamber filled with a most subtle and deadly poison extracted from a small lizard peculiar to the banks of the Upper Niger."

The point would, I saw, act just as the fang of a snake, for the thimble, when placed on the finger and pressed upon the flesh of the victim, would inject the poison into the blood, causing almost instant collapse and death. The puncture made by such a fine point would be indistinguishable, and the action of the poison, as we afterwards learnt, was so similar to several natural complications that at the post-mortem examination the doctors would fail to distinguish the real cause of death.

She held the diabolical thimble forth to us to examine, saying:

"The mode in which this was used upon the unfortunate M'sieur Thorne was undoubtedly as follows. He had seated himself at the table with his back to the door when Laumont, watching his opportunity, crept in with the thimble upon his finger, and ere his victim was aware of it he had seized him by the collar from behind and pressed the point deep into the flesh behind the right ear, at a spot where the poison would at once enter the circulation. You will remember that the doctors discovered a slight scratch behind the ear, and attributed it to having been received in the struggle which they believed had taken place. But there was no struggle. As has been proved by the medico-legist who has examined this most deadly but inoffensive-looking weapon, any one struck by it would become paralyzed almost instantly, therefore the chair was broken by him as he fell against it in fatal collapse."

"And the stolen notes? What of them?" asked old Mr. Keppel anxiously.

"Ah!" she answered. "Those accursed notes! On the following morning Laumont came to me and handed me the money, saying that as I knew the truth regarding the crime he would trust me further and give the money into my safe-keeping. I took it, for, truth to tell, I knew that he could make some very unwelcome revelations to the police regarding this place and the character of the play here. Therefore I decided that, after all, silence was best, even though I held in my possession the thimble which, I presume, in his hurry to escape from the room fell upon the floor and rolled away. I took the notes, and for some days kept them, but finding that the police were making such active inquiries I returned them to him, and he then resolved upon giving them to Miss Rosselli, either in order to further baffle the detectives or to throw suspicion upon her. He told her some extraordinary story about meeting in London, merely, of course, to put the police off the scent and cause them to believe that the money was stolen by English thieves! Soon afterwards I knew that M'sieur Cameron was aware of the manner in which his friend had been cheated here, and then, in fear of being arrested on suspicion, I fled to Russia, arranging with my friends to return here on the first of May—to-day."

"The date of your return I learnt from Laumont himself," explained Ernest, "for in the course of my inquiries immediately after the tragic affair I found that he was your associate, and in order to divert suspicion from himself he hinted at you as being the assassin."

"He denounced me, not knowing that I held this evidence of his guilt in my hand!" she cried, holding forth the finger with the curious-looking thimble upon it. "Poor M'sieur Thorne is, I fear, not the first victim who has fallen beneath the prick of this deadly instrument."

"To whom do you refer?" inquired the detective quickly.

"To M'sieur Everton, the young Englishman, who was found dead one night a year ago in the Avenue des Acacias."

In an instant the man Laumont sprang at her with all the fury of a wild beast, and clutching at her throat tried to strangle her. His eyes were lit by the fierce fire of uncontrollable anger, his dark, bushy hair giving his white face a wild and hideous look, and for an instant, in the confusion before the detectives could throw themselves upon him, it seemed as though he would tear limb from limb the woman who had confessed.

For a moment the detectives and the pair were mixed in a struggling mass, when suddenly a loud yell of pain escaped the wretched man, and releasing his hold he drew back, with his left hand clasped upon his wrist.

He staggered, swayed unevenly, uttering fierce and terrible imprecations.

"Dieu!" he gasped. "You—*you've killed me!*"

What had happened was next instant plain. In the struggle the point of his dastardly invention, which was still upon the woman's finger, had entered deeply the fleshy part of his wrist, injecting that poison that was so swift, and to which there was no known antidote.

He staggered. Two detectives sprang forward to seize him, but ere they could do so he reeled, clutched the air, and fell heavily backward, overturning the small table beside which he had been standing.

The scene which ensued was ghastly. I shall remember it through all my life.

Five minutes later, however, the wretched man who had thus brought card-sharping and murder to a fine art had breathed his last in frightful agony, his ignominious career ended by his own diabolical invention.

CHAPTER XXI
CONTAINS THE CONCLUSION

NEED I DWELL FURTHER upon the stirring events of that night? It is assuredly sufficient to say that the arrests made by the police numbered nearly forty persons, all of whom were charged with various offences, in addition to being found in an illicit gaming-house. Many of them, old offenders and desperate characters notwithstanding the fact that they were outwardly respectable members of society, in due course received long periods of imprisonment, but Julie Fournereau, in consideration of the information she had given regarding poor Reggie's death, was dismissed with a fine of two thousand francs as owner of the house in question, and has since disappeared into obscurity.

Ulrica arrived in Paris next day with Gerald, and was absolutely dumfounded when we related the whole of the amazing story. That day too proved the happiest in all my life! Need I relate how on the following morning Ernest sought me and begged me to forgive? Or how, with tears of joy, I allowed him to hold me once more in his strong arms as of old and shower hot, fervent kisses upon my brow? No. If I were to commence to relate the joys that have now come to me I should far exceed the space of a single volume. It is enough that you, reader, to whom I have made confession, should know that within a fortnight we all returned to New York by way of Liverpool, and that while Ulrica became engaged to Gerald and soon afterwards married him with the old man's heartiest approval, Ernest again asked me to become his wife—a contract which was fulfilled amid great éclat within a month of our arrival back in Washington.

Ulrica tells me that she is no longer world-weary, living only for excitement, as in those fevered days by-gone, but that her life is full of a peaceful happiness that cannot be surpassed. Nevertheless I cannot really bring myself to believe that she is any happier than I am with Ernest, for the estrangement has rendered him all the more dear to me, and we are indeed supremely content in each other's perfect love. Mrs. Thorne has returned to her home in Philadelphia, fully satisfied at having cleared up the mystery surrounding poor Reggie's tragic death, while old Benjamin Keppel, of Pittsburg, still spends his winters in rather lonely grandeur in his great white villa amid the palms outside Nice, working in secret at his ivory-turning and giving at intervals those princely entertainments for which he has become so famed in the cosmopolitan society which suns itself upon the Riviera.

As for Ernest and myself, we have not visited Nice since, for we retain a far too vivid recollection of those dark days of doubt, desperation, and despair—and of our strange and tragic meeting at The Sign of the Seven Sins.